A Word from Stephanie about Being a Winner

Everyone in my family was making a big fuss over D.J., my older sister. D.J. just won an award for getting really good grades in college. Okay, so maybe I haven't won an award in a really, really long time. But winning contests isn't everything. I mean, life isn't all one big contest. Or is it?

Thinking about winning awards got me thinking about the shiny gold President's trophy. Whoever wins the class election gets to bring it home. So I started wondering if I could win the election. Then my friend Maura started saying that I had a really good shot at winning. Before I knew it, I was off and running. Soon, everyone was saying that my campaign was the best thing to hit John Muir Middle School in years!

It looked like I was a shoo-in for class president. There was only one problem. My best friend, Allie. Suddenly, Allie wanted to run for president, too! Two best friends running against each other for the same office? I just knew it would end in disaster. I also knew I just *had* to win that trophy. Could I win the election and *not* lose Allie's friendship?

It was a big problem, all right. And not even my big family knew the answer. There are nine people and a dog in my very full house. There's me, my big sister, D.J., my little sister, Michelle, and my dad, Danny. And that's just the beginning.

When my mom died, Dad needed help. So he asked his old college buddy, Joey Gladstone, and my Uncle Jesse to come live with us, to help take care of me and my sisters.

Back then, Uncle Jesse didn't know much about taking care of three little girls. He was more into rock 'n' roll. Joey didn't know anything about kids, either—but it sure was funny watching him learn!

Having Uncle Jesse and Joey around was like having three dads instead of one! But then something even better happened—Uncle Jesse fell in love. He married Rebecca Donaldson, Dad's co-host on his TV show, *Wake Up, San Francisco*. Aunt Becky's so nice—she's more like a big sister than an aunt.

Next Uncle Jesse and Aunt Becky had twin baby boys. Their names are Nicky and Alex, and they are adorable!

I love being part of a big family. Still, things can get pretty crazy when you live in such a full house!

FULL HOUSE™: Stephanie novels

Available from MINSTREL Books

FULL HOUSE™
Stephanie

Winning Is Everything

Cameron Dokey

A Parachute Book

A MINSTREL® BOOK

Published by POCKET BOOKS
New York   London   Toronto   Sydney   Tokyo   Singapore

A MINSTREL PAPERBACK *Original*

 A Minstrel Book published by
POCKET BOOKS, a division of Simon & Schuster Inc.
1230 Avenue of the Americas, New York, NY 10020

A PARACHUTE BOOK

 Copyright © and ™ 1999 by Warner Bros.

ISBN: 0-671-01728-4

First Minstrel Books printing January 1999

10 9 8 7 6 5 4 3 2 1

A MINSTREL BOOK and colophon are registered trademarks of Simon & Schuster Inc.

Cover photo by Schultz Photography

Printed in the U.S.A.

Winning Is Everything

CHAPTER
1

◆ ◂ ◂ ◆

"For she's a jolly good fellow, which nobody can deny!"

Stephanie Tanner threw back her head and sang at the top of her lungs.

"Cut it out, Stephanie," her older sister, D.J., said with a grin. "You're embarrassing me."

"Why?" Stephanie asked. "Making straight A's in college is hard work. You deserve a song—and a party."

Every time one of the Tanners received an award, the family threw a party to celebrate. Stephanie's entire family was gathered in the living room, waiting for D.J.'s party to begin.

Stephanie and D.J. were alone in the kitchen as they loaded a tray with forks, glasses, and plates.

"I guess it's like Dad always says," Stephanie went on. "If you give something your best, you'll be surprised at what you can accomplish."

"Dad's right about that," D.J. said.

"I guess." Stephanie pushed a strand of her long, blond hair behind one ear and sighed.

"What's wrong?" D.J. asked.

"Nothing," Stephanie replied. "I guess I was just feeling like I haven't accomplished anything special in a long time."

D.J. grinned. She opened a cupboard and pulled out a stack of small dishes. "You can accomplish something special right now—you can bring Dad the cake plates!"

Danny Tanner's voice rang out from the living room. "Hey—what's the holdup in there?" he called. "Are you going to bring in those plates or not?"

Stephanie giggled. "Sometimes I think Dad can see through the walls," she whispered to D.J.

"Or read our minds!" D.J. joked back. She led Stephanie into the living room.

Stephanie set the tray on the coffee table. Her uncle Jesse and aunt Becky squished closer together to make room for her on the couch for her. Their five-year-old twins, Alex and Nicky, both tried to climb into Stephanie's lap.

Alex grabbed a cake plate. "How come Uncle

Danny lets us eat in the living room for award parties?"

"Yeah," Nicky put in. "We're *never* allowed to eat in here on normal days!"

"Award parties aren't normal," Becky answered. "They're special times."

"Right! Everybody deserves an extra-special treat when they do something great," Jesse agreed.

"And what could be more of a treat than eating cake in the living room?" Joey Gladstone joked. Joey was Danny's best friend. He had moved into the house after Stephanie's mother died to help Danny raise D.J., Stephanie, and Michelle. That was years ago. Joey was a part of the family now.

"Excuse me, everyone," Danny said. "I believe we have a celebration to begin!"

Danny strode over to the fireplace and cleared a spot on the mantel. He lifted D.J.'s dean's list certificate in its shiny gold frame.

"Ahem." Danny cleared his throat. "I know we're all incredibly proud of D.J. So let's give her a big cheer!"

"Hip, hip, hooray!" Stephanie yelled louder than anyone.

D.J.'s face flushed with pleasure. Her eyes sparkled in excitement.

She's really enjoying this, Stephanie thought. *And*

I know just how she feels. Winning an award really is special in our house!

"Speech! Speech!" Jesse called, looking at D.J.

D.J. flushed. "I just want to thank you all for my party," she said.

"You deserve it," Danny told her.

"You worked so hard for a long time," Becky added.

"Right. I'd never have the stamina," Michelle, Stephanie's little sister, put in.

"*Stamina?*" Stephanie repeated. She shot Becky a knowing look. Michelle's fourth-grade class was working on a big vocabulary unit.

"*Stamina* must be this week's vocabulary word," Stephanie whispered to Becky. "Michelle used it four times today!"

"I'm not sure I have the stamina for many more of Michelle's vocabulary words," Stephanie joked to Becky.

"Wait—I have more to say," D.J. announced. "I'd also like to say how glad I am that we could have my party *today*." She nodded at Danny.

"I'd be so upset if you couldn't be here, Dad," D.J. added. "Do you really have to leave on your trip first thing tomorrow morning?"

"I do. And thanks for reminding me," Danny told her. He grabbed a tall stack of papers from the coffee table.

4

"What's that for, Uncle Danny?" Alex asked.

"It's a list of things to remember while I'm gone," Danny answered. "And a list of your chores."

"Uh-oh. I have a bad feeling about this," Joey said.

"Don't worry," Danny told him. "It's all written down. You just have to pay attention to your assignments."

"It's going to seem awfully strange around here without you, Dad," Stephanie said.

Danny hosted a morning TV show called *Wake Up, San Francisco.* Stephanie's aunt Becky was the show's other host. They usually featured stories about people and events right there in San Francisco. But they were about to air special segments featuring other cities on the West Coast. Danny had to travel to all those cities. And his trip began tomorrow.

"Here you go!" Danny said. He passed out the first piece of paper.

Stephanie glanced at it quickly. Tops on her list was helping Michelle with homework every night. *Well, that's not too bad,* she thought.

Danny passed out a second sheet of paper. "These are copies of my schedule," he explained. "So you'll know where to reach me each day."

"Anything else?" Jesse looked impatient for his cake.

"Yes—I added phone numbers for all the hotels where I'll be staying," Danny said. "I hope you'll call whenever you need me."

"Danny, stop worrying about us," Becky said. "These lists take care of everything."

"Except the cake," Joey joked. He leaped up and sliced into D.J.'s favorite pineapple-upside-down cake. Becky helped him hand the cake around. Even Comet, the Tanners' golden retriever, got a piece.

"Oh, no!" Danny groaned as if he'd just thought of something incredibly important. "We forgot to take the picture! Stephanie, Michelle, get out of the way. D.J., stand here, by the fireplace. Have you got the camera, Jesse?"

Danny took his place next to D.J. They both flashed wide smiles as Jesse snapped their photograph.

Danny gave D.J. another hug and beamed at the family. "I'm really going to miss all you guys," he said. "Everything special will be happening without me."

"But nothing special will *be* happening while you're gone," Joey pointed out.

"That's true," D.J. agreed. "I'll be taking a rest from all my schoolwork."

6

"And I'll be busy, doing your work *and* mine down at the station," Becky said.

"While I'm running around, looking after the twins," Jesse added.

"Well, I have my big soccer tournament," Michelle said. "That's special to me."

"To me, too," Danny told her. "You can tell me all about it over the phone," he promised. He turned to Stephanie. "How about you, Steph? Anything special going on at school?"

"The class elections are coming up," Stephanie began. "I thought I'd write something special about them for *The Scribe*."

The Scribe was the newspaper at John Muir Middle School. Stephanie was one of their top reporters. She also worked for Scribe TV, the new television station at the school.

"What special things are you going to write?" Danny asked.

"Well, I thought I'd write about how each candidate could improve things at school if elected," Stephanie replied.

"Didn't you already write a story like that?" D.J. asked.

"Sure, I remember it," Becky chimed in. "It was very impressive, Stephanie. Your ideas were great."

"I always said Stephanie would be a terrific class officer," Danny added. "Like D.J."

D.J. had been president of her junior class in high school.

"Remember the party we had when D.J. won her election?" Jesse asked.

"We'd have just as big a party for Stephanie," Becky said.

"But I'm not running for office," Stephanie pointed out.

Danny frowned. "I don't know why not," he said.

"I bet you could win, Steph," D.J. agreed. "If you gave it your best shot."

"We could even help," Jesse said. "Michelle and I could paint your campaign posters."

"I could help with your speeches," Becky said in excitement.

"It's a great idea, Stephanie! The kids at school already respect your opinion," Danny added. "You owe it to them to run for president."

Stephanie held up her hands, laughing. "Okay, okay! I get the point. You all think I should run."

"We don't *think* it," Danny corrected her. "We *know* it!"

Hmmmm, Stephanie thought. She pictured her campaign poster: *Elect Stephanie Tanner Class President!*

"Maybe I *should* give it a shot," Stephanie said.

"Sure you should," D.J. encouraged her. "Winning the election would be a really big accomplishment, Steph."

"If you have the stamina," Michelle added.

Stephanie laughed. "Right, Michelle."

Danny began clearing an extra space on the mantel. "Why are you doing that, Dad?" Stephanie asked.

"Because the class president brings home a big, shiny trophy," Danny replied. "I'm making room for your trophy."

"I haven't won the election yet," Stephanie reminded him. "I haven't even decided to run."

But it's not such a bad idea, she thought. *In fact, running for class president might be the most special thing I've done in a long, long time!*

CHAPTER
2

◆ ◄ ◆ ◆

"Oh, no!" Stephanie cried the next morning. "I overslept!" She stared at her alarm clock and groaned. "Wake up, Michelle. We're late for school."

Stephanie scrambled out of bed. She didn't bother with her bathrobe. Instead, she snatched up the clothes on the back of her desk chair.

Danny always insisted the girls lay out their school clothes the night before. It was one of those things that usually drove Stephanie crazy. But now she was glad he did it.

On the other side of the bedroom, Michelle sat up. "We can't be late. Today's the day of my big vocabulary test. How could Dad forget that?"

"Dad didn't forget," Stephanie answered. "He isn't here, remember? He left early this morning."

"Oh, right," Michelle said. "Hey, wait a minute. I need the bathroom first."

"No way!" Stephanie called. She was already halfway down the hall. "You know the rules," she added. "Whoever gets there first gets the bathroom."

Stephanie quickly brushed her teeth and washed her face. Then she raced back to her room and pulled her clothes on. She gave her hair a quick brush, then pulled it back in a scrunchie.

"I hate being late," she muttered as she sprinted downstairs. "Now I don't even have time for breakfast!"

"Hey, Stephanie!" Joey called as he saw her streak by. "What about breakfast?"

"Too late," Stephanie called back. "No time!"

She snatched her backpack up from the front hall table and pulled open the front door.

"Stephanie," Joey shouted. "Catch!"

Stephanie spun around just in time to catch the granola bar Joey tossed out.

"You're a lifesaver," Stephanie called as she hurried out the door. "Thanks!"

"Maura, wait up!" Stephanie waved one arm at Maura Potter as she raced down the hall.

Maura's brown hair whipped across her face as she whirled around. "You're late," she declared.

"I know! I can't believe I missed homeroom!" Stephanie exclaimed.

"Well, you're just in time to meet Darcy and Allie before first period," Maura told her. "They're in the office."

"The office?" Stephanie asked. "What are they doing there?"

"I don't know." Maura shrugged.

Maura was the newest member of their group. Stephanie had been best friends with Allie Taylor since kindergarten. Darcy Powell became their other best friend when she moved to San Francisco in sixth grade.

Stephanie first met Maura when they were in elementary school. They were friends for a while. Then they drifted apart until Maura started working at Scribe TV. After a few misunderstandings, Stephanie and Maura became friends again.

"Boy, you're really out of breath," Maura commented. She shoved her glasses up her nose and squinted at Stephanie. "What did you do, run all the way to school?"

"Practically," Stephanie admitted. "I didn't hear my alarm go off."

"I thought your dad always gets you up," Maura commented.

Stephanie unwrapped her granola bar and took

a huge bite. "Usually he does," she said. "But he left for Seattle today."

"Seattle is famous for its coffee bars," Maura said. "They have the best chocolate cappuccinos anywhere."

"Naturally, you'd know that," Stephanie teased. Maura always knew what was trendy. She was the most artistic and offbeat of the four friends.

They joined the steady stream of students hurrying down the halls of John Muir Middle School. They reached the office and leaned back against the wall to keep out of the way.

"You sure can tell it's Monday, can't you?" Maura said. "Half the people here don't have their eyes open yet." She shot Stephanie a glance. "Sort of like you."

"I'm not *that* sleepy," Stephanie protested.

"Okay, what color scrunchie is in your hair this morning?" Maura asked.

"Scrunchie? What scrunchie?" Stephanie joked. She stole a glance in the shiny glass of the trophy case outside the office.

"Just for the record, the scrunchie is blue," Stephanie said.

"You cheated!" Maura protested. "I saw you check your reflection." She gazed into the trophy case. "Wow. I never paid much attention to these trophies before. There must be fifty of them. Debate, speech, football—they're so big and shiny!"

"But the fanciest one is for class president," Stephanie said. "My family thinks I should run for office this term."

"Really? Then, read this!" Maura grabbed Stephanie's shoulders and turned her to face a poster on the office door.

YOU CAN BE PRESIDENT the poster read. SIGN UP TODAY! In the center of the poster was a picture of the gold president's trophy.

"Then, you think I *should* run?" Stephanie asked.

"Definitely," Maura said. "You're very active around school. You're a *Scribe* reporter and you work for Scribe TV. Everyone knows you, Steph."

"But just because people know me doesn't mean they'd vote for me," Stephanie pointed out.

"But you have more going for you than that," Maura went on. "Remember when you wrote that article about how the whole school should try harder to recycle paper? Everyone *did* try harder. You really know how to make people get active. That's what we need in a president. I only wish we thought of this sooner!"

"Really?" Stephanie felt more and more excited.

"Sure. You're a cinch to win," Maura said. "All you need is some great publicity. Like a really amazing campaign slogan. Something that shows you're perfect for the job."

"Any ideas what the slogan should be?" Stephanie asked.

"We'll figure that out *after* you decide to run," Maura teased. "What do you say?"

Stephanie gazed at the president's trophy. *It seems like everyone thinks I can do it*, she thought. *They'd all be so proud of me if I won.*

"Yes!" Stephanie declared. "I'm convinced."

"Then, you'd better sign up," Maura said.

"Let's go!" Stephanie flung open the office door. She and Maura pushed their way inside.

"Stephanie!" Darcy exclaimed. She and Allie were just on their way out.

"Hi, guys!" Stephanie greeted them. "Guess what?" She rushed on before anyone could answer. "Maura thinks I could win class president. All I need is a great campaign slogan. Any ideas?"

Allie and Darcy exchanged looks of surprise. "When did you decide this?" Allie asked.

"Just now," Stephanie answered. "Why?"

"Well, uh, because you couldn't possibly be ready for the Meet-the-Candidates assembly tomorrow afternoon," Allie replied.

"There's an assembly tomorrow?" Stephanie frowned. "That doesn't give us much time to come up with a slogan. Or anything."

"Not if we want to do something special," Maura agreed. "All I can think of are the boring things. Like making posters, handing out flyers, shaking hands, and stuff."

"Steph, wait a minute," Allie said. "I'm going to—"

"You're right, guys," Stephanie interrupted. "That stuff *is* boring."

"You need a good gimmick for tomorrow," Maura agreed.

"Stephanie," Allie tried again. "Wait, please. I know you have a lot of school spirit and all, but—"

"That's it!" Maura cried. "We'll play up your school spirit! You can wear green and yellow to the assembly."

"I look terrible in yellow," Stephanie protested.

"Stephanie! Listen to me!" Allie commanded.

Stephanie stared at her in surprise. "What's wrong?" she asked.

"You *do* have a lot of school spirit," Allie said. "But this election isn't about school spirit. Or great gimmicks. It's about picking the best candidate for the job of president. You haven't even mentioned any of the issues."

"You know I care about school issues," Stephanie said. "But I can't do anything about them until I win the election, right? So, first, I have to sign up. Where's the sign-up sheet?"

"Here it is!" Maura handed the sheet to Stephanie, who signed it without looking. Maura took it back and read it. "Great. Only two other candidates! Sam Baldwin and . . ." Her voice trailed away.

"And who?" Stephanie asked. She bent over the list herself. "And . . . Allie Taylor!"

Stephanie stared at Allie in shock.

"That's what I was trying to tell you," Allie said. "I just signed up. I'm running for class president, too!"

CHAPTER

3

♦ ◄ ◢ ♦

Stephanie swallowed hard. "You, Allie—*you're* running for class president? Against *me?*"

"Why shouldn't I?" Allie demanded. Her cheeks flushed bright pink.

"I didn't mean it that way," Stephanie protested. "It's just that . . . well, you never said anything about it before."

"I didn't know before today," Allie said. "Darcy just convinced me this morning."

"And, Steph, *you* never mentioned running either," Darcy pointed out.

"Well, I just decided, too," Stephanie said.

"I don't know what to say," Allie told her. "You're the one who always told me I should get more involved in school activities. And I really do care about the issues."

"Allie could make a big contribution," Darcy added.

"Well, yeah, but—" Stephanie began.

"Cool it for a minute," Maura broke in. "There's a major case of pink approaching."

Stephanie paused as a group of Flamingoes walked by the office. She definitely didn't want them to catch her arguing with her friends. It would be all over school by lunchtime.

The Flamingoes were a group of popular, and snobby, girls. They always wore the latest styles—in pink. Today they had on identical fuzzy pink angora crop tops over black leggings. Rene Salter, their leader, even wore pink patent leather boots.

The Flamingoes always looked great. But they could also be mean. They'd given Stephanie and her friends a hard time for years.

Nobody said another word until the Flamingoes were out of earshot.

"Whew!" Maura exhaled. "Those pink outfits are enough to make anyone support school uniforms."

"Yes! That's what I mean!" Allie said in excitement. "Everybody's always saying we should convince the school board that uniforms are bad. But

19

if we had uniforms, the Flamingoes couldn't go around showing off their fancy new outfits."

"And making fun of kids who can't afford fancy clothes," Darcy added.

"Right," Allie said. "They couldn't even wear pink every day."

"They'd probably wear pink underwear or something," Darcy joked.

"Ahem!" Stephanie cleared her throat loudly. "Can we get back to the subject, please? What are we going to do about the election? I mean, Allie and I are best friends. We can't run against each other. That would be terrible."

"Yeah. You'd force all your friends to choose between you," Darcy agreed.

"It could be worse than that," Maura pointed out. "You might split the vote."

"What does that mean?" Darcy asked.

"She means that if Allie and I compete, the kids who like us both won't know who to support," Stephanie explained.

"She's right!" Allie exclaimed. "And if the vote gets split, we'd *both* end up losing."

"And Sam Baldwin would get elected." Maura moaned.

"We can't let Sam win," Darcy said. "He's brand new at John Muir. He doesn't know anything yet."

"But he's pretty popular already," Maura told

her, looking a little worried. "Everybody thinks he's cool since he's from Los Angeles. He could be tough to beat."

"All the more reason to run the right candidate against him," Allie said.

"Exactly. But who's the right candidate?" Darcy asked.

There was an uncomfortable silence.

"Let's be logical about this," Maura finally said. "The person who beats Sam has to be really well known at Muir. Which means that person should be involved in activities that reach all different kinds of students."

"That sounds like you, Steph," Allie admitted.

"They should also be really committed to the issues," Darcy added. "They should care about the school, and want to change it for the better."

"That sounds like you, Al," Stephanie said.

"Well, they should also have a great personality," Darcy added. "They'd have to be really outgoing to beat a guy like Sam."

"That's Stephanie," Maura remarked.

There was another awkward silence. The warning bell rang for first period.

"I'd better go," Allie said. She lowered her eyes, looking away from Stephanie.

"I should go, too," Stephanie replied. She had history next. Her classroom was in the opposite direction from Allie's. "I, uh, guess I'll see you later, Al," she said.

"Yeah. Later," Allie muttered. She and Darcy hurried down the hall.

"Wow," Maura murmured. "I had no idea you and Allie would be running against each other."

"Me, either," Stephanie said. "She really wants to run. But so do I."

"Maybe Allie will change her mind," Maura said. "No offense, but she isn't nearly as outgoing as you, Steph. Not nearly as many kids know her around school."

"Yeah," Stephanie muttered. "Do you think she'll drop out?"

Maura shrugged. "I wouldn't be surprised. Allie doesn't really like giving speeches, does she?"

"Not really," Stephanie agreed. "And she'll have to do a lot of public speaking for this campaign."

"Right. So maybe Allie will think about it today, and change her mind. Running for office isn't really like her."

"It isn't," Stephanie agreed. "I wonder if you're right, Maura. I wonder if Allie will drop out after all."

"Wait and see," Maura suggested.

"Right," Stephanie replied.

She headed to her history class. This was going to be a long day. She didn't know how she was going to survive waiting to find out what Allie would do.

I wish Dad were around, she thought. *He'd know exactly how I should handle this. He could give me the perfect advice. Oh, well.* Stephanie sighed. *One way or the other, I guess this will all be settled by tonight.*

But nothing *was* settled.

Allie skipped lunch, and headed straight to the library with Darcy after school. No one said anything about her dropping out of the campaign.

Stephanie felt more and more upset. When the phone rang that evening after dinner, she nearly leaped out of her chair to be the first to answer.

"Dad!" Stephanie cried into the phone. "I'm so glad you called," she went on. "I really need to talk to you!"

"I'm glad I called, too," Danny said. "I can't believe how much I miss everyone already."

"I really miss you," Stephanie said. It was so great to hear his voice.

Michelle tugged on Stephanie's sleeve. "Hurry up!" she nagged. "Just because you got here first doesn't mean you get to hog the phone."

"Shhh," Stephanie hissed at her. "Go clear the table, Michelle. It's your turn tonight."

"What's going on?" her father asked.

"Nothing, Dad," Stephanie answered. "Michelle wants to talk to you."

"Tell Michelle she'll get her turn," Danny said. "I scheduled plenty of time for everyone. The schedule is on my handout sheet. You didn't lose it, did you?"

"Of course not," Stephanie answered. "We posted one right here, on the refrigerator door."

"Good," Danny said. "I don't have much time, honey. So tell me what happened in school today. Are you running for class president?"

"Yes! And that's what I wanted to talk to you about," Stephanie eagerly began. "You see, Allie—"

"That is so great," Danny interrupted. "I know it's the right decision, Steph. It's the perfect way for you to get even more involved at school."

"I know, Dad. But, see, I'm a little worried because—"

"Oh, just trust your instincts," Danny answered. "I know being president is a lot of responsibility. But I'm sure you can handle it."

"Dad, you don't understand," Stephanie tried again. "See, there's a big assembly tomorrow. To meet all the candidates. And Allie is going to—"

"An assembly, huh? What you need is a great way to introduce yourself to the voters," Danny said. "Something that will make you stand out from the crowd."

"I know that, Dad. But, I—"

"No 'buts' about it," Danny told her. "You should ask Becky to help you. And D.J. I bet they both have terrific ideas for running a unique campaign."

Buzzzz!

A loud noise rang in Stephanie's ear. "Ouch!" she exclaimed. "What was that awful buzzing?"

"That's my timer," Danny told her. "Which means it's now Michelle's turn to talk. Sorry, honey."

"But, Dad!" Stephanie cried. "I didn't even get to tell you about Allie and—"

"Now, Steph, it's no fair hogging the phone," Danny told her. "I'll speak to you again tomorrow. And I'll expect a full, detailed report on your assembly! Good luck!"

Stephanie sighed. "Thanks, Dad." She held out the phone to Michelle. "Your turn," she said.

So much for getting the perfect advice, Stephanie thought. *I'll have to try to talk to Dad again tomorrow. But for tonight, I guess I'm on my own.*

CHAPTER
4

♦ ◂ ▸ ♦

"Maura! Finally, you're home!" Stephanie nearly cried with relief into the telephone. "I was beginning to think I was the only person on the planet."

"Why would you think that?" Maura's laugh echoed in the telephone. "You mean, nobody in your whole family is home?"

"Just about." Stephanie flopped back onto D.J.'s bed. She was using the private line in her sister's room. "D.J. is out with friends. Uncle Jesse's busy with the twins. Aunt Becky has to work late every night while my dad is away. Even Michelle is busy, studying her vocabulary words."

"I guess this means you didn't get through to Allie or Darcy either," Maura commented.

Stephanie hesitated. "Darcy's line was busy," she answered. "And, well . . ."

"You're not sure how to talk to Allie, right?" Maura asked.

"Right," Stephanie said. "You didn't hear that she dropped out yet, did you?"

"I didn't," Maura replied.

"Me either," Stephanie said. "This is so weird. I mean, Allie always helps me plan things. But I can't ask her to help on *my* campaign. Not if she's planning *her* campaign."

"No. And it's like Darcy is on Allie's side," Maura added. "So you can't really talk to her either."

"That's exactly how I feel," Stephanie said.

"Well, you've still got me," Maura told her. "I know you're in a rough spot, Steph. But we can try to straighten things out with Allie tomorrow. In the meantime, we've got to plan your first public appearance."

"I guess so," Stephanie said.

"Sure," Maura told her. "You can't disgrace yourself at the assembly tomorrow afternoon."

"You're right," Stephanie agreed. "And I still need a slogan, and a gimmick. And I have absolutely no idea what I should do."

"Well, people love to get things for free," Maura

said. "So maybe you need some kind of giveaway. Something you can pass out at the assembly."

"It should be something that will remind people of me," Stephanie said.

"How about things that start with the same first letter as your name?" Maura suggested.

"What else starts with S?" Stephanie asked.

"Soap. Soda. Salamanders," Maura recited.

"That's a big help," Stephanie said. "I can just see me passing out bars of soap."

"You could pass out cans of soda," Maura suggested.

"Way too expensive," Stephanie said. "We need something smaller, and cheaper. Like M & M's or something."

"They don't have an S." Maura pointed out. She paused. "But Skooters do!"

"Skooters! Those little colored candies—what a great idea!" Stephanie exclaimed.

"And even better if you use only the green and yellow ones—for our school colors!" Maura giggled.

"Maura, you're a genius," Stephanie told her. "That is just what we need!"

A knock sounded on D.J.'s door. *Who could that be?* Stephanie wondered. "Who is it?" she called.

The door opened and Nicky poked his head in. "Stephie, come play superheroes with me," he said. "I need someone to rescue. And Mommy's not home yet."

"I can't play now," Stephanie told him. "But come in and show me which superhero you're playing."

Nicky's face lit up. He bounded into the room.

Stephanie chuckled. "Maura, I wish you could see this," she said into the phone. "Nicky's wearing his Superman pajamas and a towel tied around his shoulders for a cape."

"I'm Super Nicky!" he announced.

"You do look super," Stephanie told him. "But why don't you go rescue your dad? I'll play with you later."

Nicky pouted. "I already rescued him. But okay." He ran out of the room. His cape flapped behind him.

"He sounded so cute," Maura said. "You're really Super Stephanie to the twins, aren't you?"

"That's it!" Stephanie shouted.

"What's it?" Maura asked. "The fact that I'm now completely deaf in one ear?"

"No," Stephanie replied in a softer voice. "That's my slogan! Super Stephanie!"

"Now *you're* the genius," Maura exclaimed in excitement. "I can see our posters and banners. 'For a Super President, Vote for a Super Candidate. Super Stephanie'!"

"Yes!" Stephanie cheered. "We are really on a roll! I can't wait to tell Allie and Dar—" Her voice trailed away. "Oh. I guess they won't want to hear my brand-new slogan."

"Cheer up," Maura said. "You and Allie will be fine. I mean, it's only an election. You're still best friends."

"You're right," Stephanie replied. "Allie's been my best friend forever. One election can't change that."

"No way!" Maura told her. "Listen, we have a ton to do to get ready for tomorrow!"

"You're right," Stephanie said. "Right now we need to concentrate on one thing and one thing only—Operation Elect Super Stephanie!"

CHAPTER
5

"Wow! My table looks amazing!" Stephanie stepped back to admire the bright green and yellow crepe paper draped over her information table in the cafeteria. "Thanks so much, Maura. I never could have done this without you!"

"No problem." Maura glanced at her watch. "Last period starts in two minutes!" she exclaimed. "We finished just in time for the Meet-the-Candidates assembly."

"I'm glad they're going to let in only two classes at a time," Stephanie said.

"That's so kids can get a chance to meet all the candidates and ask any questions they have," Maura explained.

"Right. I remember from last year," Stephanie

told her. "Only last year it was Ricky Collins running for president. And this year it's me. I can still hardly believe it."

Maura grinned. "Believe it. Here—have some Skooters to calm your nerves."

She reached for the big blue mixing bowl in the center of the table. Stephanie had borrowed it from home that morning. It was filled to the brim with green and yellow Skooters.

"It looks good, doesn't it?" Maura asked. "And our table fits right in. It goes with the way the election committee decorated the rest of the room."

She waved her arm around the cafeteria. Green and yellow streamers hung from the ceiling. Green and yellow balloons were taped to the walls.

Stephanie glanced around. All of the candidate information tables formed a circle in the center of the room. A sign on the wall announced: MEET THE CANDIDATES!"

"Nervous?" Maura asked.

"Yeah." Stephanie nodded. "But I'm excited, too."

The door to the auditorium flew open. The first two classes came rushing in.

"Steph!" Maura said suddenly. "We forgot to hang your slogan banner!"

"Hurry!" Stephanie cried. "We don't have much time!"

Stephanie snatched up the banner she'd painted late the previous night. She hardly even heard the other candidates around her as she and Maura taped the sign to the front of the table.

Stephanie stepped back and admired her campaign slogan: FOR A SUPER PRESIDENT, VOTE FOR A SUPER CANDIDATE—STEPHANIE TANNER.

"And now, for the finishing touch," Maura said.

She opened her backpack and pulled out a green sweatshirt decorated with a big yellow *S* on the front.

"No way!" Stephanie exclaimed.

"If you're going to say you're the super candidate, you have to look like the super candidate," Maura declared. "Come on, put it on."

"Where's my cape?" Stephanie teased as she took the sweatshirt.

"Don't laugh yet," Maura warned. "I'm working on it."

Stephanie pulled the sweatshirt on over her head.

"I'm not so sure this is a good idea," she joked. "Once they see me, the school board is going to insist we get school uniforms for sure."

Stephanie struck a modeling pose. She spun around and took a few steps, as if she were walk-

33

ing down a runway at a fashion show. "How do I look?" she asked, glancing back at Maura.

"Steph! Watch out!" Maura cried. She pointed over Stephanie's shoulder.

"Huh?" Stephanie asked. She backed right into another table. The table slid back a few inches. A big cardboard sign teetered and fell onto the floor.

Stephanie gasped. "Oh, I'm so sorry!" she cried. She bent down and lifted the sign. It was painted on white posterboard with large black lettering: VOTE FOR ALLIE TAYLOR—SHE KNOWS WHAT'S IMPORTANT!

Below the lettering was a list of all the issues facing John Muir students.

Stephanie's heart began to pound. She glanced up—straight into Allie's face. Darcy was standing next to Allie.

"Allie!" Stephanie felt her face turn red. "Sorry. I didn't mean to bump your table."

"Right," Allie answered quietly. She took the sign from Stephanie's hands. "I noticed that you and Maura were ignoring us all day."

"We weren't ignoring you," Stephanie protested. Though it was true—she *had* been ignoring her. All day she'd been waiting and hoping to hear that Allie decided to drop out of the election.

"I . . . I thought maybe you wouldn't go through with it," Stephanie stammered. "You know. Maybe you'd decide not to run."

Allie's eyes flashed. "Why would I decide that?"

"I don't know!" Stephanie glanced around, feeling awkward.

This is terrible, she thought. *Here I am, afraid to talk to my best friend!*

"Don't you think my campaign ideas are good?" Allie demanded. She pointed to her list of school issues.

"No, I'm sure they're good," Stephanie replied. "It's just that, well, I know how much you hate public speaking. That's all. I thought you'd get nervous about giving speeches and stuff and change your mind. And maybe drop out."

"No," Allie said stiffly. "That's not true. You *wanted* me to drop out. I tried to tell you I wouldn't, but you didn't even listen to me."

"I *did* listen," Stephanie insisted. "I know you care about stuff, Al. But you are kind of quiet and shy sometimes. I thought the campaign thing would flip you out."

"I will *not* flip out," Allie declared, looking more insulted than ever.

The room roared with sound as more students filed into the cafeteria.

"Steph, Allie," Maura murmured. "You guys should chill out. People are staring."

Stephanie couldn't take her eyes off Allie's face. Her cheeks were bright pink, the way they got when she was really upset or embarrassed. She looked more determined than Stephanie had ever seen her.

"I'm sorry about this, Stephanie," Allie said in a low voice. "I tried to call you last night, but your line was busy."

"I was talking to Maura. But I wanted to call. I called Darcy, but I guess she was busy talking to you," Stephanie replied.

"Why shouldn't she talk to me?" Allie demanded. "Darcy is my friend. She promised to help me with my campaign before you ever signed up to run. You make it sound like she was going behind your back or something."

"I didn't say that!" Stephanie exclaimed.

"Come on, you guys," Maura broke in. "Don't fight. We're all friends, remember?"

"We *are* friends," Darcy agreed.

"Friends support each other," Allie argued. "They don't tell you that you're too quiet and shy to run for election."

"I didn't say that," Stephanie protested. "I just thought that campaigning is better for someone who's more outgoing. You know, livelier—"

"Wait a minute," Allie interrupted. "Are you saying that I don't have a personality?"

"No!" Stephanie exclaimed. "That didn't come

36

out the way I meant it. Of course you have a personality, Allie."

Allie chewed her lip. Then she stared straight at Stephanie. "Yes, I *do* have a personality," she said. "And I'm not dropping out. I really care about the issues. I care about having school uniforms or not. And I care about the idea of having students grade their teachers. I want to run for president."

Stephanie stared from Allie to Darcy and Maura and back. "Well . . . I'm not dropping out either," she said. "I want to win, too."

"Well, then," Allie began. Her voice shook a little. "I guess there's only one thing left to say."

"What?" Stephanie asked.

"May the best candidate win." Allie turned and marched behind her table. Darcy helped her set up her campaign sign.

Stephanie hesitated. Then she nodded to Allie. "You're right," she said. "May the best candidate win."

CHAPTER
6

◆ ◀ ◢ ◆

"Stephanie, are you sure this is a good idea?" Maura whispered, crouching down behind a huge bayberry bush.

"Absolutely," Stephanie whispered back. "It's the perfect use for the green cape you made."

"I made it so you could wear it," Maura pointed out.

"This idea is much better," Stephanie assured her. "You saw how much everyone loved my school spirit campaign at the Meet-the-Candidates assembly the other day. They were way more into our gimmicks than Allie's boring talk-about-the-issues campaign."

"Or Sam Baldwin's 'Sam the Man' buttons," Maura added.

Stephanie and Maura crouched by the entrance to John Muir. It was early Thursday morning, before most students arrived for the day.

But it was the perfect time to pull off Operation Flagpole, the first stunt in Stephanie's campaign.

"So far, so good," she whispered. She checked her watch. "Thirty seconds to Mr. Coombs."

Mr. Coombs was the John Muir Middle School custodian.

"I can't believe I let you talk me into this," Maura complained. "If we get away with it, you get all the glory. If we get caught, I get all the blame."

"We're not going to get caught," Stephanie said. "Mr. Coombs opens the front doors at the same time every day. Then he goes straight to the flagpole."

"How can you be so sure?" Maura asked.

"Because I've seen him," Stephanie said. "On all the days I come in early to do Scribe stuff. Don't worry, I've timed this perfectly."

"Quiet! I think I hear him!" Maura exclaimed.

Stephanie heard a squeak as the heavy front door of the school opened, then closed again. Next she heard the jingle of the custodian's keys.

Stephanie kept her eyes on her watch. "Five, four, three, two, one," she counted softly.

"Get down!" Maura whispered.

They ducked behind a big camellia bush. Stephanie peeked out from between its branches, watching as the custodian walked over to the flagpole.

"Morning, Mr. Coombs," a voice called out.

"Good morning, Susan," the custodian replied.

"I told you so!" Stephanie whispered triumphantly.

"Shhhh!" Maura hissed.

Susan Allen hurried up the steps and into the school. She was one of Scribe TV's gutsiest reporters. Stephanie often competed with her for the hottest stories. Susan always came to school early to work on Scribe TV stuff, a fact Stephanie was counting on this morning.

Mr. Coombs raised the flag to the top of the flagpole. Then he went back inside, too.

The second she heard the door slam, Stephanie stood up.

"Go!" she told Maura.

Clutching the green cape in one hand, Maura sprinted for the flagpole.

Stephanie watched as Maura lowered the flag again, being careful not to let it touch the ground. Then she tied the green cape to the line below the flag.

"Hurry," Stephanie called. "Susan will be back out here in about two seconds!"

Maura tied one final bow. Frantically, she pulled

on the rope to run the flag back up to the top of the pole.

Just beneath it, a bright green cape with a big yellow *S* snapped in the morning breeze.

"Time's up. Run!" Stephanie shouted.

Maura scampered back to the camellia bush. She got there just seconds before Susan burst out the front door.

She carried a portable video camera on one shoulder. She dashed to the bottom of the steps and stopped.

"Oh, man, this is totally great," Susan murmured. "What a story!"

Susan lifted the camcorder, turned it on, pointed it at the flagpole, and began to speak into the built-in microphone.

"And there you have it, Muir voters. A terrific campaign stunt from Stephanie Tanner. An anonymous tip to the Scribe TV office put this reporter on the scene. When I came to school, not five minutes ago, this flagpole looked normal. Now, as you all can see, something has changed."

"Hey," Maura whispered. "Is she trying to say you're not normal?"

Stephanie stifled a giggle. "Who cares? Don't you know there's no such thing as bad publicity?"

Susan continued her on-the-scene report.

"It seems there's no stopping Tanner when it

comes to outrageous attention getters. First, free candy during the Meet-the-Candidates assembly. Now a Super Stephanie flag in school colors. It's plain Tanner has more school spirit than any other person running. I guess that's why she's called the Super Candidate."

Stephanie turned to Maura and gave her a silent high-five.

"This is Susan Allen for Scribe TV, live in front of John Muir Middle School."

Stephanie and Maura grinned at each other as Susan went back inside.

"Operation Super Stephanie is definitely high-risk," Maura said.

"Yeah," Stephanie answered. "But you know what? It's also definitely working!"

She turned to hurry into the building. And found herself staring at Allie and Darcy.

Ulp!

She took a deep breath. "Uh, hi, guys," she said. "What are you doing here so early?"

"I had an appointment with Susan Allen. To do an interview for Scribe TV," Allie replied. She glanced up at the green cape flapping in the breeze. "I guess you *don't* need to make appointments. Or do stuff like regular people."

Stephanie stiffened. "This is an election, Allie. I'm just trying to get the voters' attention."

"There are better ways than this," Allie said.

"Calm down, Allie," Maura told her. "It's a great stunt. Admit it. I bet you're just jealous. You wish you thought of it yourself, right?"

Allie flushed and grabbed Darcy's arm. "Come on, Darce. We'll be late." They hurried into the building.

Stephanie felt a knot form in her stomach as she watched them go.

"Don't worry about it," Maura told her. "Just keep thinking about winning the election. Picture that shiny gold trophy in your home!"

Right, Stephanie thought. *Dad will be so proud when he sees that trophy. And so will I!*

"Wait a minute," Stephanie said to Joey that evening. "You mean we're having spaghetti *again?*"

"We had that last night," Michelle complained. She opened the fridge, took out yogurt and a banana, and dumped them into the blender.

"What are you doing?" Joey asked.

"Making a fruit smoothie," Michelle answered.

Nicky and Alex padded into the kitchen.

"Can we help?" Alex asked.

"Sure," Michelle said. "In a minute."

"And macaroni and cheese the night before that," Stephanie added. "Are we ever going to have something that doesn't have noodles in it?"

"Hey, give me a break, you guys," Joey said. "I'm not as good at this as Danny is."

Danny had assigned the cooking duties to Joey. Usually, D.J. would help, but Danny had also given D.J. the week off to relax.

Stephanie groaned. "I wish I got home early enough to help cook," she told Joey. "But I've been busy with this election every day this week."

"I'm doing my best," Joey said.

"But for three days in a row we've had Twinkies for breakfast, peanut butter and jelly for lunch, and pasta for dinner," Stephanie complained.

Joey peered into a big pot of steaming water. "Right! And I think I'm starting to get the hang of this boiling-water thing," he said.

He dropped the lid onto the pot with a bang.

Stephanie shook her head. "You know what, Joey?" she suggested. "You should branch out. Maybe we could have rice tomorrow instead?"

"No way," Joey objected. "Danny's notes say cooking rice is hard—you ruin it if you take the lid off too soon. That would never work for me. I like to look in there and see what's going on."

The telephone rang. "Dad!" Stephanie exclaimed.

Michelle lunged for the phone, but Stephanie got there first. She snatched up the receiver.

"Hello?"

"Hi, Steph! How's my president-to-be?" Danny asked.

Stephanie felt her spirits lift. "Dad, I have so much to tell you," she began. "Because this thing with Allie has really got me—"

"I know you've lots to tell," Danny interrupted. "But I have a big surprise."

"What is it?" Stephanie asked.

"My next assignment is in San Diego. I have to go past San Francisco to get there. So I get to come home for a few days," Danny said. "I should be there the end of next week."

"That's great!" Stephanie cried.

"What?" Michelle demanded.

Stephanie ignored her. "That means you'll be home right after the election," she said.

"Is something wrong?" Danny asked. "You don't sound as excited about it as you did a couple of days ago, honey."

"That's what I'm trying to tell you," Stephanie said. "It's about Allie. You see, she's running for— oh, no!" she yelped.

A burst of steam shot out of Joey's pot. Boiling water poured over the sides and hissed as it hit the hot burner.

"Joey, your pot is boiling over!" Stephanie yelled.

"Can I help now, Michelle?" Alex asked. He reached up and switched on the blender.

"Alex, no!" Michelle cried. "I didn't put the lid on yet!"

The blender whirled, shooting yogurt and bananas across the kitchen.

"Help!" Alex wailed. A huge glop of yogurt landed in his hair and began dripping down his face.

Stephanie dashed over and turned the blender off.

"What's going on here? What's the matter?" Jesse dashed into the kitchen and picked up Alex. "What a mess!"

Yogurt covered the entire countertop and splattered across the cabinets. Chunks of banana slid off the counter and landed on the floor with a soft *plop*.

"Hello? Anybody? What's happening?" Danny's voice squawked from the receiver.

Joey leaped for the stove. "Pot holders," he cried. "I need pot holders!"

Michelle snatched two pot holders from their magnets on the side of the fridge. "Here," she said, handing them over.

Joey grabbed them and quickly pulled the pot off the stove. Stephanie held her breath while he placed the steaming pot in the sink.

"Gee," Joey said. "I guess I'm not as good at boiling water as I thought."

"Stephanie!" Danny repeated. "What is going on?"

Joey winced. "Uh-oh."

Stephanie lifted the phone again. "Um, nothing, Dad," she said. "Joey's spaghetti water boiled over and Alex made a little mess with the blender."

"Put Joey on," Danny said.

"It's no big deal, Dad," Stephanie assured him. Danny was the neatest man in the world—he was obsessed with cleaning.

Dad would flip if he saw this mess, she thought.

"Stephanie," Danny answered. "Please put Joey on right now."

"Okay," Stephanie said. "Sorry," she whispered as she handed Joey the phone.

"Hey, Danny," Joey said, trying to sound cheerful. "How's it going?"

Stephanie helped Michelle finish setting the table. She could tell from Joey's expression that Danny was lecturing him.

"Yes, Danny," Joey said. "Yes, kitchen safety is very important. Yes, I know."

"I hope Dad doesn't forget about talking to the rest of us," Michelle said.

"I'm sure he won't do that," Stephanie reassured her. "You know how organized Dad is. He'll lecture Joey for three minutes and thirty-three seconds, then tell him his time is up."

"Okay, Michelle, your turn," Joey called.

"There, see?" Stephanie said. "What did I tell you?"

Michelle sprinted for the phone.

"Boy," Joey said. "Being away sure makes Danny worry a lot. He would never get so upset about a pot of water if he was home."

"You're right about that." Stephanie sighed as she finished setting the table.

She'd never get a chance to talk to her dad about her problem now. And she had to do something about Allie—soon.

Stephanie set down a glass with a thump. *What am I waiting for?* she asked herself. *It's my problem. So I have to find a way to solve it.*

And the best way to do that was to talk to Allie.

She glanced at her watch. The phone would be free in exactly seven minutes and forty-three seconds.

I'll call Allie tonight, she decided. Tomorrow was Friday. She could ask Allie, Darcy, and Maura to come over tomorrow after school. They could talk everything out then.

There had to be a way for both of them to run for president—and still be friends!

CHAPTER
7

♦ ◀ ♦ ♦

"Whew!" Maura collapsed onto Stephanie's couch. "Thank goodness it's Friday!"

"You said it," Stephanie agreed. "No campaigning for two whole days. What a relief!"

"Don't forget the speeches next week," Maura said. "You have to be prepared for that. You should work on your speech this weekend."

Stephanie groaned. "You had to remind me! I was hoping to catch up on my *Scribe* work tomorrow. Ever since the election campaign started, I haven't had time to work on any new story ideas."

"Maybe I could help you," Maura offered. "We could brainstorm after Allie and Darcy go home."

Stephanie checked her watch. "I wonder where they are, anyway? It's getting late."

"I know," Maura agreed. "So, how did Allie act when you invited her?"

"I think she was glad I called," Stephanie replied. "She said she wanted to talk, too."

"Really? Then why didn't she sit with us at lunch today?" Maura asked. "We could have talked then."

"I guess she wasn't ready yet," Stephanie said. "And it is kind of public in the cafeteria. I feel better keeping this whole thing private."

Maura slowly shook her head. "I never guessed how much this campaign would come between you guys," she said.

"I know," Stephanie told her, fiddling with the sleeve of her sweater. "I never guessed it would even get in the way with Darcy."

"Darcy feels trapped in the middle," Maura pointed out. "I never meant for either of us to have to take sides."

"I know you didn't." Stephanie sighed. "I've been racking my brain all week. And I still can't come up with a way out of this mess."

The doorbell rang. Stephanie jumped up from the couch. "That must be them now!" she exclaimed.

"Hi," Allie said as soon as Stephanie opened the door. She lowered her eyes and stared at the ground, as if she weren't sure what to say next.

"Hi, Steph. Thanks for asking us over," Darcy said.

Stephanie felt her stomach tense up. Things had never been so awkward with Allie and Darcy before!

I hate this! she thought. *I almost wish I weren't part of this whole campaign!*

"Come in," she said.

Darcy and Allie followed Stephanie back into the living room. Everybody settled on the couch.

Allie sat on one end, Stephanie on the other. Darcy and Maura sat between them.

What do I say now? Stephanie wondered.

A few minutes ticked by. Nobody said anything.

This is awful, Stephanie thought. *I can't stand this silence! But what should I say first?*

"So," she finally said. "Uh, I'm really glad you guys could come over tonight." Her voice squeaked and she cleared her throat. "I, um . . ."

Allie was so uncomfortable, she turned and looked over her shoulder. She suddenly gasped. "What *happened?*" she cried.

Stephanie turned to see what Allie was looking at.

Michelle stood in the living room doorway. She was wearing her soccer uniform.

At least, Stephanie thought it was the soccer uniform. It was hard to tell for sure.

"Michelle—what are you wearing?" she asked.

Michelle glanced down at her uniform. It was so shrunken and wrinkled that Stephanie couldn't even see the big number on the front of the shirt.

"I'm wearing a disaster," Michelle answered. "Of astronomical size."

"Astronomical" was Michelle's latest vocabulary word.

"What will I do?" Michelle wailed. "This uniform is so tight, I don't think I can run in it. How will I play soccer today?"

"Didn't your dad do the laundry?" Maura asked.

"No," Michelle told her. "Uncle Jesse is doing laundry while Dad's away. He shrunk my uniform. And he left it in the dryer all week, trapped under Joey's giant tennis shoes."

Maura giggled.

Michelle tugged on her uniform top, trying to stretch it over her stomach. The minute she let go, it popped up again.

"Can't you wear something else to your game?" Stephanie asked.

"No, it's a tournament," Michelle replied. "The rules say you have to be in uniform. If I don't wear it, my whole team will be out of the tournament."

"It's not so bad, Michelle," Stephanie tried to comfort her.

"It *is*," Michelle insisted. "Even if it wasn't so tight, there's no way the rest of my team can play if I look like this."

"Why not?" Darcy asked.

"Because they'll be on the ground—laughing," Michelle answered. "I'm a total mess! Even my socks have wrinkles."

"At least he didn't get your shoes," Allie joked.

Michelle giggled. Stephanie shot Allie a grateful look. Poor Michelle really needed cheering up.

"Maybe you'll start a whole new uniform style," Allie added.

"She's right," Maura put in. "Who knows? It could be a cool new trend."

Michelle shook her head. "Nice try, guys."

Jesse appeared in the living room, jingling his keys. "All set to go?" he asked Michelle.

He stopped short when he caught sight of her. "Um, Michelle," he said slowly. "Is your uniform supposed to look like that?"

Michelle rolled her eyes. "Think about it, Uncle Jesse."

Jesse winced. "I don't understand what went wrong," he said. "I followed Danny's laundry instructions to the letter."

"But you forgot to take my uniform out of the dryer and iron it," Michelle told him.

"Iron it?" Jesse winced.

53

"Dad always irons my uniforms," Michelle said.

"I could iron it now," Jesse offered.

"There's no time!" Michelle headed for the front door. "Come on, Uncle Jesse," she said over her shoulder. "I don't want to be late for the most *astronomically* embarrassing event of my entire life."

Jesse hurried after her. He closed the door with a thud.

"That was pretty strange," Maura commented.

"Yeah," Darcy said.

Another awkward silence followed.

This can't go on, Stephanie thought.

She took a deep breath. "Listen, you guys, I've been thinking," she began.

Briiing!

The doorbell rang, cutting her off. Stephanie got up to answer the door.

"Not another interruption," Darcy cracked.

"Well, at least we know one thing," Maura joked.

"What?" Allie asked.

"Stephanie's been thinking!" Maura laughed.

"Very funny," Stephanie called as she pulled open the front door.

"Pizza for Stephanie Tanner," the guy on the doorstep announced.

"Pizza?" Stephanie repeated. "I didn't order any pizza."

The guy shrugged. "It says your name right here." He handed her a receipt. "It's already paid for."

"Um, okay," Stephanie said. "Thanks."

She took the pizza box and headed back to the living room. "Look, you guys!" she called. "Someone sent me a pizza. Who could it be?"

"Who cares?" Maura said. "It smells great."

"It smells just like pepperoni, my favorite," Stephanie said. "It has to be from someone who knows me."

"Why don't you open it, Steph?" Allie suggested. "Maybe the explanation's inside."

"Oh, right, spelled out on top of the pizza in olives or something," Stephanie said.

She set the pizza box down on the coffee table and lifted the lid. A puff of fragrant steam wafted up.

"Hey, wait a minute," she exclaimed. "You're right, Allie. Look at this!"

Stephanie held up the box. On top of the pizza, spelled out in pepperoni, was a big letter *S*.

"That's your campaign symbol," Maura exclaimed. "Somebody sent you an Operation Super Stephanie pizza!"

"But who? And why?" Stephanie asked.

"Maybe to show their support," Allie said in a quiet voice. "To show they know that you're the number-one candidate for class president."

Stephanie set the pizza back down. "*You* sent it, Allie. Didn't you?" she asked.

Allie stood up. "Yes, I did," she said. "I wasn't sure how to tell you, but I'm withdrawing from the race. I'm not running for president anymore."

"I don't understand," Stephanie said. "Why drop out now?"

"I can't compete against you, Steph," Allie said. "Those campaign stunts you've been pulling are too good. Besides, I was afraid this competition would ruin our friendship for good."

"Oh, Allie! Nothing could do that," Stephanie protested. She threw her arms around Allie in a big hug. "I'm so sorry I hurt your feelings. I should never have said that stuff about you being too shy to run."

"That's okay," Allie told her.

"No, it isn't," Stephanie said. "And I'm really sorry."

"I'm just glad we're talking again," Allie said. "I hated not talking to you all week."

"Me, too!" Stephanie admitted. "It was terrible. I really missed talking things over with you."

"And I didn't know how to talk to you about *not* talking to you!" Allie exclaimed.

"So you let the *pizza* do the talking," Maura joked. Everybody cracked up.

Allie grinned. "Not a bad idea, huh?"

"It was a completely awesome idea," Stephanie said. "I wish I'd thought of it!"

"Actually, I think you did," Darcy remarked. "Passing out candy with an *S* already on it was a great idea, Steph."

"Maura thought of that," Stephanie told her.

"Hey—we make a great team," Darcy said.

"Well, maybe now that we're not competing, Darcy and I could help with *your* campaign," Allie suggested. "If that's all right with you," she quickly added.

"Of course it's all right!" Stephanie cried. "I'm so glad we can be friends again!"

Allie grinned.

"Deciding to drop out must have been really tough, Allie," Maura commented.

"It was," Allie agreed. "I do think I have a lot to contribute. But maybe not as president."

"Wait a minute," Stephanie declared. "I am just about to be totally, completely brilliant!"

"Uh-oh. Stand back, everybody," Darcy teased her. "We're in the path of a Tanner brainstorm!"

"Let's hear it," Maura commanded.

"What's the one thing that every president needs?" Stephanie asked.

"A bottle of aspirin?" Darcy joked.

"No," Maura countered. "A lifetime supply of Skooters!"

"You guys are flunking," Stephanie said. "And the answer is so obvious."

"So what is it?" Maura asked.

Stephanie slung an arm over Allie's shoulders. "The one thing every president needs is a good vice president," she declared. "And I know just where I can find one."

Allie sucked in her breath. "You want me to be your running mate?" she asked.

"Absolutely!" Stephanie said.

"This is definitely one of your better brainstorms, Steph," Maura said.

"I wish we thought of it before," Darcy declared.

"Sure. It's perfect," Maura added. "If you run as a team, you can both win. And you won't split the votes!"

"And with both of you running, Sam Baldwin doesn't stand a chance," Darcy added.

"Who do you think Sam will pick for his vice president?" Allie asked.

"No one knows," Darcy said. "But whoever it is, they won't be as great a team as Tanner and Taylor!"

"That's the spirit!" Stephanie cried. She held out

her hand to Allie to make it official. "Running mates?"

"Running mates," Allie declared, shaking on it.

Darcy and Maura whistled and cheered.

"My first act as your new running mate is to make a motion," Allie announced.

"Let's hear it," Stephanie commanded.

"I move we eat this pizza before it gets cold!" Allie grinned.

"I definitely second the motion," Maura said.

Stephanie dove for the pizza box. She handed out steaming slices of Super Stephanie pizza.

"A toast!" Maura said.

"Quick," Allie cried. "My cheese is sliding off."

"All for one—" Maura started.

"And one for all!" they all finished together.

"Okay, you guys," Stephanie said as soon as they settled down again. "Finish eating. We have only one week left to campaign. But with Allie and Darcy helping, we can come up with *twice* the gimmicks! So let's get started and see who can come up with the most ideas."

CHAPTER
8

◆ ◀ ◆ ◆

"Stephanie! What did you *do* to this place!" D.J. walked into the kitchen and stopped still in amazement.

Stephanie lifted her head off the kitchen table and groaned. "I know, I know," she said. "It's a mess, right?"

"A mess?" D.J. repeated. "It's a disaster!"

Stephanie glanced around the room. Open cartons of cereal sat in the middle of the table. Empty Twinkie boxes covered the top of the refrigerator. The sink was piled high with dirty dishes. The door to the dishwasher hung open. More dirty dishes sat inside, because no one had remembered to run the machine the night before.

"Steph! Why didn't anyone clean up in here?" D.J. asked.

"Well, Becky's hardly been here," Stephanie answered. "She's been going to work early and staying late every night. So she couldn't clean up."

"What about Uncle Jesse?" D.J. asked. She checked the work schedule on the refrigerator. "He had kitchen cleanup twice."

"Yes, but the twins are running him ragged and he just didn't have the energy to clean," Stephanie replied. "And Joey's been spending every second buying groceries and trying to put meals together. So that leaves me and Michelle."

"So?" D.J. asked. "What's wrong with you and Michelle?"

"We're doing our best," Stephanie replied. "But Michelle has a giant vocabulary test this week. I can't get her to do anything."

"That leaves you," D.J. pointed out.

"I know," Stephanie told her. "But I have only two days until the election! I can't stop to clean up the kitchen."

D.J. frowned.

"I know—it's my house, too," Stephanie agreed. "But I'm all out of stunt ideas for my campaign. And Allie and I really need to come up with something major!"

"Maybe you should stop focusing on stunts," D.J. suggested. "When I ran for class president, I tried to focus on the issues. Have you finished your speech for tomorrow?"

"Are you kidding?" Stephanie gestured around the messy kitchen. "How can I write a speech in this mess?" She sighed. "Really, Deej. I'll never complain about Dad being a neat-freak again."

"What does that have to do with your speech?" D.J. asked.

"I don't know," Stephanie admitted.

"I know little things have been going wrong," D.J. began. "But—"

"Little things?" Stephanie interrupted. "On Monday, Joey tried to make baked potatoes in the oven. He didn't know you were supposed to poke them with a fork first. So they blew up."

"That's too bad, Steph, but—" D.J. tried again.

"But that's when I was working on my speech," Stephanie went on. "And my notes got thrown out when we cleaned up the mess."

"But that was Monday! This is Wednesday," D.J. pointed out. "You could have redone your speech by now."

"No, I couldn't," Stephanie protested. "Because yesterday Alex and Nicky spilled poster paint all over the living room carpet. I spent half the night cleaning it up."

"Steph, I hate to say this, but it sounds like

you're making excuses," D.J. told her. "You're not avoiding the speech, are you?"

"Why would I do that?" Stephanie asked. "I'll do my speech—as soon as I come up with more campaign stunts. Really, Deej, I have it all planned out. I'll begin talking about the school uniform issue. And then make a tough argument that we ought to be able to evaluate teachers, because the high school kids do."

"That sounds good," D.J. said.

"Right. I told you I know what to say," Stephanie said. "School uniforms are good, and so is grading teachers. It's simple."

"Okay, you convinced me," D.J. said. "How about this. I'll help you clean up this mess. And if I get any great ideas for your campaign, you'll be killing two birds with one stone."

"Sounds good to me." Stephanie stood and stretched. "Let's tackle the dishes first."

Two hours later, Stephanie and D.J. stepped back to admire the gleaming kitchen.

"Thanks, Deej," Stephanie said. "I never could have done this alone."

"I'm sorry I didn't come up with any great ideas for your next stunt," D.J. apologized.

Just then they heard Becky's car pull into the driveway.

"Hey, Aunt Becky's home early!" Stephanie cried.

"Great," D.J. said. "She can help you with your stunt ideas. Becky's great at that stuff." D.J. glanced at her watch and yawned. "I promised myself a long, hot bath tonight," she told Stephanie.

"Go ahead," Stephanie told her. "I'll get Aunt Becky to help with my campaign."

Stephanie waited for Becky to trudge into the kitchen.

"Hi, Steph," Becky said with a tired smile. "Pull out a chair for me, huh? I'm moving so slowly, I'm practically walking backward."

"You look really tired. You should sit down," Stephanie told her. "And I'll fix you something to eat."

"That sounds great," Becky replied.

"How about I heat up leftovers from the Golden Wok?" Stephanie asked.

She pulled Chinese takeout cartons out of the refrigerator.

"You mean Joey didn't cook it? Good," Becky said. "That means it's actually safe to eat."

She sat down at the kitchen table and eased her shoes off. Then she folded her arms on the table and rested her head on them.

Stephanie piled some food on a plate and stuck

it into the microwave. She poured out a glass of juice and set it beside Becky.

"Stephanie, you're an absolute lifesaver," Becky murmured.

"Well, I do have a sneaky motive," Stephanie confessed. "I'm hoping you'll help me dream up some fresh campaign stunts for the next two days. I'm having trouble, and it's our last shot at grabbing the voters."

"Anything," Becky answered. "Just let me get my second wind."

Stephanie pulled the Chinese food from the microwave and placed it on the table.

"So, how are things going at work?" she asked.

Becky didn't even lift up her head. "We're so busy! I've never been this exhausted!" she answered. "I really miss Danny. We all tease him for being so organized, but he sure does get things accomplished."

"Tell me about it!" Stephanie said.

"I never realized half the stuff he did around the studio until he wasn't there to do it anymore," Becky continued. "Now every time I turn around, there's something new I haven't done. It's hard to catch your breath in a situation like that."

Stephanie nodded, thinking about her dad. He always kept the household running so smoothly. And he usually ended up doing most of the cooking. And the laundry. Both of which had been total disasters since he'd left.

"I know what you mean," Stephanie said. "I can't wait for Dad to come home. Only three more days!"

She gave the Chinese food a few good stirs and pushed the plate across the table toward Becky.

"Here you go," she said. "Nice and hot!"

Aunt Becky was sound asleep.

Wow! Stephanie thought. *She really meant it when she said she was tired!*

"Hey," a voice from the kitchen door called. "What's going on in here?"

"Uncle Jesse, shhhh," Stephanie whispered.

Jesse tiptoed into the kitchen. His face was concerned as he looked at his sleeping wife.

"Don't worry about it," he whispered back. "She's just trying to avoid Joey's cooking."

"Nice try, Uncle Jesse," Stephanie whispered back. "But I heated up leftover Chinese."

"I guess I'd better get her up to bed," Joey murmured. "I hate to wake her, but I can't let her spend the night at the kitchen table."

Very gently, he woke Becky and led her upstairs.

Stephanie put the food back into the takeout boxes.

So much for getting help from Becky, she thought.

She crossed the room, lifted the phone, and dialed Maura's number. Maura answered on the second ring.

"Steph!" she cried in excitement. "I've got it! I thought of the perfect stunt for tomorrow!"

"Fantastic!" Stephanie exclaimed. "Tell me all about it."

"Sure—but first, tell me how your speech is going," Maura said.

"It's totally under control," Stephanie told her. "School uniforms: good. Grading teachers: good."

Maura laughed.

"Right," Stephanie said. "Don't worry about my speech. I'm great at making speeches and thinking on my feet. Tell me your idea."

She listened as Maura described everything.

"Maura, you are a lifesaver, and a genius!" she said. "And after tomorrow, there's no doubt about it. I'm going to win that election and be president. Nothing can stop me now!"

CHAPTER
9

◆ ◢ ◣ ◆

"Time to settle down, everyone!" the student council adviser, Mrs. Booth, announced. "I know we all want to hear the speeches of our presidential candidates—Sam Baldwin and Stephanie Tanner."

Stephanie wiped her sweaty hands on her plaid miniskirt. She glanced around from her seat in the front row. The auditorium was packed with students.

"First to take the stage, Sam Baldwin and his running mate, Mark Latz," Mr. Bird said.

Stephanie watched nervously as Sam and Mark climbed onstage. A loud burst of applause and cheers and whistles greeted them.

"Great," Allie muttered. "Just what we need. The Sam Baldwin fan club!"

"A fan club!" Stephanie whispered back. "Now, why didn't I think of that?" She giggled.

"Next, will Stephanie Tanner and her running mate, Allie Taylor, take their places," Mrs. Booth called.

"Okay, running mate, this is it," Stephanie said. She and Allie walked up onto the stage.

"Go Super Stephanie," a voice from the crowd yelled out.

Stephanie smiled and waved. She felt totally confident, just thinking about the little surprise she and Maura cooked up on the phone last night. Not even Allie and Darcy knew about it.

Stephanie just hoped Maura had been able to get everything they needed before school this morning.

"Stephanie won the coin toss," Mrs. Booth announced. "So she'll speak first."

She signaled for Sam, Mark, and Allie to join her in the row of chairs at the back of the stage.

Stephanie stepped up to the microphone.

"I'd like to thank you all for coming today," she said. "This is a really great turnout. But then, we're a truly great school, and I'm part of an outstandingly great class."

Stephanie's classmates hooted their approval. Stephanie spotted Maura standing in the wings offstage. Maura gave her a thumbs-up sign.

"I could spend a lot of time up here talking

about school uniforms and grading teachers. But most of you already read my articles in *The Scribe*. You know I'm in favor of those things."

Stephanie paused and gazed over the audience. "So instead, I'd like to take the time to tell you how glad I am to see so many of you here. It really shows a lot of school spirit. And I think we need more spirit days to show our commitment. In fact, I think we should show a little school spirit right here and now!"

Stephanie pointed at Maura. That was Maura's cue to set off the big surprise. She nodded to Maura, who was waiting in the wings.

Stephanie held her breath as Maura yanked on a rope. The rope was attached to a bag hanging high over the stage.

Maura pulled again and the bag opened. Dozens and dozens of green and yellow helium balloons were released from the bag. They floated out over the audience.

The students in the auditorium went wild.

"Super Stephanie! Super Stephanie!" they chanted. Groups of kids batted the balloons around.

Stephanie stepped out from behind the microphone and took a bow.

Well, that's that, she thought.

Her speech was short. But the audience was definitely on her side.

It was better to quit while she was ahead.

"Thank you," she said when the applause died down. "Now I'll turn the microphone over to my opponent, Sam Baldwin."

Stephanie walked to the back of the stage and sat next to Allie. "Whew!" she said. "I'm glad that's over."

"I should have known you'd come up with some wild stunt," Allie whispered. "But, Steph, you didn't take anywhere near your full time. There's all kinds of stuff you didn't even mention."

"Stop worrying, Allie," Stephanie whispered back. "Even Sam Baldwin liked it. He was laughing."

Sam stepped up to the microphone. "I really have to hand it to Stephanie," he said with a smile. "She sure does know how to set up a great publicity stunt. I couldn't even begin to match her."

Several people in the audience applauded.

"But then, I'm not so sure I want to," Sam went on, speaking over the noise of the crowd. "I think there should be more to a presidential candidate than flashy stunts. I think a candidate should know about what's really going on at John Muir."

Stephanie blinked. *Of course I know about things at John Muir,* she thought. *Everyone already knows I do!*

"But we haven't heard about the issues from the

Super Candidate," Sam went on. "She hasn't put any energy into talking about what John Muir students really care about. All her energy has gone into gimmicks. Maybe that's because the Super Candidate doesn't know what the issues really are."

"Uh-oh," Allie muttered under her breath. "Here it comes."

"Don't worry," Stephanie told her. "Everybody *loved* my stunt. And they hate long speeches."

Allie didn't answer.

"And what about some of these stunts?" Sam continued. The audience was silent now. Sam really had their attention.

A knot formed in the pit of Stephanie's stomach. *I know I did the right thing,* she tried to convince herself. *Kids hate long speeches. And they loved the balloons.*

Besides, she had written about the issues lots of times before.

"Take the incident with the flagpole," Sam went on. "I agree it showed a lot of spirit, but am I the only one who wonders about how a Scribe TV reporter just happened to be there at the time? I'm not accusing my opponent of doing anything wrong. But isn't she also a Scribe TV reporter? I think that's an awfully big coincidence. Don't you?"

Sam paused. A low murmur rose from the audience. Stephanie could see heads start to nod. The knot in her stomach got a little tighter.

This can't be happening, she thought. *He's twisting everything around! He's making it sound like I'm dishonest!*

"I'd like to talk about an issue facing John Muir students," Sam said. "I'd like to talk about school uniforms."

Some of the kids in the audience applauded. Stephanie chewed nervously on her lip.

"I'm totally against them," Sam was saying. "If the school board makes us wear uniforms, we'll lose our right to express our individuality. We'll all be clones. We'll be like robots in a bad science fiction movie."

That's not true, Stephanie thought. *School uniforms are good! Allie thinks so, too!*

Stephanie knew she'd have another chance to return to the microphone. She and Sam each had one more turn to speak. She'd be able to argue against anything Sam said that she really disagreed with.

I can do that, she told herself. *I can think on my feet.*

"In closing, I challenge my opponent to explain her exact position," Sam said. "I think she owes it to you. A good candidate has to take a stand on what's really going on. If she can't, well, I'm sure you all know who to vote for. Thank you."

The audience applauded as Sam sat down.

Stephanie stood up. Her heart started pounding. She plastered a cheerful smile on her face as she walked back to the microphone.

This is easy, she told herself. *I'm not beaten yet. I can still win the election.*

If ever she was going to think fast on her feet, the time was now. The election was tomorrow—if she didn't gain the voters' confidence now, she had no chance.

"I'd like to thank my opponent for bringing up some of the more serious issues facing us," Stephanie said into the microphone. "I know what they are. And I'm not afraid to comment more on my own opinions."

Just as soon as I figure out what I could possibly say!

Stephanie stared out at the faces in the crowd. Her mind was a total blank. Her heart raced even faster.

What do I think? What can I say? she thought in a panic.

"Excuse me, Stephanie!"

Startled, Stephanie turned to find Allie standing right behind her.

"I wonder if I could say a few words, as your running mate," Allie said.

Stephanie's stomach stopped churning. She wasn't in this alone. Allie was going to help her!

"Of course," Stephanie said, hoping she didn't look as relieved as she felt. She turned back to the audience.

"I'm happy to share the microphone with Allie Taylor, my vice president," she said. "I'm sure you all remember Allie was running for president herself, but she decided she'd rather join my campaign. And I think it's important for you to hear from both of us."

Stephanie shot a quick glance over at Sam Baldwin. Sam was frowning, and Mark looked nervous. Obviously, Sam's running mate wasn't going to get anywhere near the microphone.

Stephanie took a deep breath. She had stumbled badly, it was true. But there was still a chance she could come out on top. With Allie's help, of course.

"Please welcome Allie Taylor," she finished.

Stephanie stepped aside so Allie could take the microphone.

"Thank you, Stephanie," Allie said. She looked out over the audience. "I agree with Stephanie. I don't want to make a long speech either. I know how boring those are."

The audience laughed. Stephanie felt her spirits lift still further. Allie just might pull this off!

"Sam did a great job bringing up the issue of

school uniforms. But I think saying we'll lose our individuality is too easy. It might even be an insult to our intelligence.''

Wow! Stephanie thought. *Allie's really going for it.*

''Haven't we all had at least one moment when we were embarrassed by what we looked like? When we wished people could see beyond what was on our outsides? Of course we have,'' Allie went on.

Stephanie stole a glimpse out at the audience. They were following Allie's speech closely, waiting to see where she was going.

''I know this might not be a popular opinion,'' Allie admitted. ''But Sam said it himself. A candidate shouldn't be afraid to face the issues. So I'm not going to back down.''

A few kids nodded. Stephanie crossed her fingers.

''Besides, I trust your intelligence,'' Allie said. ''I know you'll understand me when I say that wearing uniforms doesn't have to make us less individual. Because if we look more alike outside, it could be easier to see what we're like *inside*. That's what truly makes us individuals. Not our clothes.''

This is totally fantastic, Stephanie thought. *I never knew Allie had it in her.*

Stephanie leaned over to the microphone. ''Isn't she awesome?'' she asked the crowd. ''I'm sure you can see why I wanted Allie to be my running mate."

The audience burst into applause. Stephanie captured Allie's hand and raised it high in the air.

"Way to go, partner," she called out. "She'll be a great vice president, don't you think?"

The kids in their class started cheering. The girls stepped back from the microphone to thunderous applause.

Top that, Sam Baldwin, Stephanie thought happily.

But all the way back to her seat, she had to ignore the little voice in the back of her mind.

The voice that whispered Allie would be more than just an awesome vice president. She'd be a totally awesome president.

CHAPTER
10

◆ ◀ ▶ ◆

"Ooooh," Stephanie moaned the next morning. "My stomach hurts."

"You'll feel better when you eat something," D.J. said, following Stephanie down the stairs.

At the thought of food, Stephanie's stomach lurched.

"I wouldn't be so sure about that," she declared. "I don't have hunger pains—I have butterflies! I'm surprised I'm not airborne."

D.J. patted Stephanie's shoulder. "Today's the day of the election, isn't it?"

"Gee, how did you guess?" Stephanie said. She stared at the mantel on her way past the living room. The butterflies in her stomach began flying faster.

"I've got to bring home that president's trophy for the mantel, Deej," she said. "I've just got to."

"I'm sure you will," D.J. replied.

"I wish Dad were here," Stephanie added, heading into the kitchen. "I know he'd help me get a grip."

"And I'll bet I know how," D.J. said. Stephanie knew exactly what she meant.

"Super-deluxe-extra-energy muffins," she and D.J. said at the same time.

"They taste great, but they sure do look ugly," Stephanie commented.

"That's because they've got everything but the kitchen sink in them," D.J. said.

"I wish we knew how to make them."

"You expect Dad to reveal one of his secret recipes? No way!"

"You're right." Stephanie smiled. "What was I thinking?"

"What's for breakfast?" Michelle asked. She walked into the kitchen with Alex and Nicky right behind her.

"I don't know," Stephanie said. "I haven't even seen Joey this morning."

"Never fear," Joey cried, bursting through the back door. He held up a brown paper bag.

"Did you just come from the store?" D.J. asked.

"Yeah. We had no food left in the fridge," Joey

said. "Danny assigned the shopping to Becky, but she hasn't had time to get to the grocery store." He emptied the bag onto the kitchen table. "Breakfast is served."

"Joey," Stephanie protested. The table was covered with packages of sweet junk food. "We can't eat that for breakfast."

"Speak for yourself," Michelle answered, reaching for a package of cupcakes. "I can."

"But it's so bad for you," Stephanie protested. "You'll get sick."

"No way," Joey said. "I've been eating this stuff for breakfast all my life, and look how I turned out."

Stephanie rolled her eyes at D.J. "I rest my case," she said. "Things sure are different with Dad gone."

"You can say that again!" Michelle reached enthusiastically for her second package of cupcakes.

"Ooohhh." Stephanie was still moaning later that afternoon. She was more nervous than ever. She put her head down on her desk and moaned again. "I think I'm going to be sick!"

Students had been voting all day long. Stephanie and her friends waited nervously in the student council room.

"The election results will be announced on Scribe TV any minute," Maura said.

Darcy wrapped an arm around Stephanie's shoulders. "Come on, snap out of it, Steph. The Super Candidate can't cave in now."

"Not even under Super Pressure!" Maura added.

"I don't think it's the pressure." Allie chuckled. "I think it's all the campaign candy she's been eating."

"I didn't mean to eat it. I meant to pass it out," Stephanie explained. "You know, one last re- minder to vote for Super Stephanie. But I was so nervous, I kept eating it myself. And to think I turned down solid food for breakfast."

"With Joey cooking? What was it?" Darcy asked.

"My choice of Ho-Hos, Sno Balls, or Twinkies," Stephanie mumbled.

"What, no fruit pies?" Maura joked.

The bell rang. An excited silence settled over the room. Stephanie sat up straight. She couldn't face the election results with her head on her desk. After all, she was still the Super Candidate.

Mrs. Booth, the student council adviser, switched on the TV monitor at the front of the room.

The screen came into focus, showing four report- ers, one from each class. They were sitting at a long desk. Behind them was a banner that read STUDENT ELECTIONS.

Stephanie reached out to link hands with Allie on one side and Darcy on the other. Maura grabbed hold of Allie's other hand.

"This is it, you guys," Stephanie said. "If I don't make it through this, thanks for everything."

"Calm down, Steph," Darcy said.

The election was going to be close. Stephanie could just feel it. She and Sam Baldwin had both run good campaigns.

One by one, the reporters read the election results. Stephanie barely listened to the other class elections. All she could think about was how great it would feel to tell her dad she won the election.

All of a sudden, Susan Allen's voice broke into Stephanie's thoughts.

"And the winner in the close race between Stephanie Tanner and Sam Baldwin is—"

Susan tore open a large, official-looking envelope. "Stephanie Tanner and Allie Taylor!" she cried.

"Allie, we did it!" Stephanie yelled.

Mrs. Booth presented Stephanie with the gleaming gold president's trophy. "You can keep this in your house now," she told her. "At the end of your successful term, we'll have your name engraved."

"I can't wait," Stephanie told her.

"Congratulations, Steph!"

Stephanie turned to find Darcy and Maura behind her. She threw her arms around them and gave them each a big hug.

"I can't believe it," Maura exclaimed. "Operation Super Stephanie is a total success!"

"I never could have done it without you guys," she said.

Other students crowded around Stephanie and Allie to offer their congratulations. Even Sam Baldwin came to shake Stephanie's hand.

"Whew," she said as she gathered up the books for her next class. "Thank goodness the hard part is over. Now things can get back to normal around here."

"Normal?" Allie cried. "Steph, have you gone completely nuts? We've just been elected. This is when the hard part *starts!*"

"Oh, I know that," Stephanie said quickly. "But now we just have to go to student council meetings twice a week. It won't be nearly as hard as campaigning every single day."

Allie looked doubtful. "I think being president is a lot of work," she said slowly.

"Of course, Allie. But we can lighten up now!" Stephanie cried. "I'm just so glad we won the election. I can't wait to tell my dad. And I'm going right home to do it!"

Thirty minutes later, Stephanie burst through the

front door of her house, waving the president's trophy in the air.

"Dad, I won!" she shouted. "I won!"

Stephanie dashed into the living room. Danny was nowhere to be seen. But Michelle and D.J. jumped up when she entered the room.

"Quick, help me dust this space on the mantel for my trophy," Stephanie told them. "I want it to be the first thing Dad sees when he walks into the room."

Michelle looked up, her expression gloomy.

"Steph," she said, "Dad's not coming."

CHAPTER
11

◆ ◢ ◣ ◆

"Not coming?" Stephanie echoed. "What do you mean, Dad's not coming?"

"He got some kind of last-minute assignment," D.J. answered. "He can't make it home after all."

Stephanie dropped down onto the couch beside her sisters. She tried to swallow her disappointment. She couldn't.

"But I won the election! He *has* to be here," she wailed.

D.J. gave her a sympathetic look.

To Stephanie's surprise, Becky walked into the living room. It was the first time her aunt had been home before dinner in days.

"I'm sorry about your dad, Steph," she said. "When I found out he couldn't come, I decided to leave the studio early in case we had great news to celebrate. Looks like we do," she added, gesturing toward the trophy.

Stephanie nodded. "Thanks, Aunt Becky," she said.

She really appreciated the extra effort her aunt was making. But, somehow, it just wasn't the same. No celebration was going to be the same without Danny.

The telephone rang.

"I'll bet that's Dad," Michelle said.

Stephanie picked up the receiver. "Hello?" she said.

"Steph?" Danny's voice came across the line.

"Hi, Dad," Stephanie said, trying to make her tone as upbeat as she could. She knew her father must feel terrible about not coming home.

"So?" Danny pressed. "Give me the good news."

"I won," Stephanie said. "I really did. I'm looking at the president's trophy right this second!"

"That's fantastic!" Danny cried. "I'm sorry I can't be there to celebrate like I hoped, honey. Something came up at the last minute."

"That's okay, Dad," Stephanie said, swallowing a giant lump in her throat. "I understand."

"Is everybody there?" Danny asked. "I think it's about time we did some singing."

Stephanie glanced over her shoulder. The rest of

the family had come into the living room while she was talking to her dad.

Seeing everybody else made Stephanie feel a little better. Her family was making a big effort to celebrate.

"We're all here," she told her father.

"Okay, hold the phone out so everybody can hear me," Danny said.

"He wants to lead the singing," Stephanie whispered, raising the phone in front of the others.

Aunt Becky chuckled. "That's our Danny."

"One, two, three," Danny's voice called.

The family burst into "For She's a Jolly Good Fellow." Stephanie put the president's trophy in the very center of the mantel.

"Is the award on the mantel? How does it look?" Danny asked when the singing ended.

"It looks just great, Dad," Stephanie said. *But it would look even better if you were here*, she thought.

"I have to go now," her father said. "I'll call again as soon as I can. Congratulations, honey. I'm very proud of you."

"Thanks, Dad," Stephanie said. She hung up the phone. A strange silence filled the living room.

Now that the phone call from Danny was over, nobody seemed to know what to do next. This wasn't anything like the family's usual celebrations.

"Well," Uncle Jesse said. "I have some stuff I need to do in the studio. Come on, Joey."

"Good going, Steph," Joey called as he followed Jesse out.

"Come on, monsters," Becky said to the twins. "You can help me cut Stephanie's ice cream cake."

"All right!" Alex and Nicky exclaimed.

"I know it's not as meaningful as a cake your dad might make," Becky said to Stephanie. "But I got them to make it with your favorite ice cream, chocolate butter almond."

"Thanks, Aunt Becky. I really appreciate it," Stephanie said.

Aunt Becky and the twins headed into the kitchen. Stephanie, Michelle, and D.J. sat back down on the couch.

"Well," Stephanie said. "I guess that's that."

She stared at the president's trophy on the mantel. There it was, her very own award.

It just didn't look right.

"I don't know what's the matter with me," Stephanie confessed. "I should be so excited. But I'm not. Dad was supposed to be here to help me celebrate. It isn't the same when he's gone."

"I bet I know just what he'd do if he were here right now," D.J. said.

"What?" Stephanie asked.

"He'd be giving you one of his special 'I'm proud of you, honey' hugs."

"That always makes me feel better," Michelle put in.

"On three," D.J. instructed. "One, two, three!"

Michelle and D.J. threw their arms around Stephanie and squeezed tight.

"No more!" Stephanie protested, laughing. "I'll pop."

"I told you that would make you feel better," Michelle said.

"It does," Stephanie admitted. "Thanks, you guys."

The sisters sat in silence for a moment.

"Oh, come on," D.J. finally said. "This moping has to stop. Dad wouldn't like it. Besides, look on the bright side."

"Bright side?" Stephanie echoed.

"Yeah, what bright side?" Michelle asked.

"Well," D.J. said. "For once, we made it through a phone call from Dad without a major household disaster. He didn't get into a panic and think he had to rush right home."

Stephanie sat up straight.

"What did you just say?" she asked.

"Watch out," Michelle said. "Stephanie's got that look on her face."

"Be quiet, Michelle," Stephanie commanded. "Deej, say that again."

"All I said was nothing bad happened when Dad called this time," D.J. said. "So he didn't freak out and think he had to rush right home."

D.J.'s eyes widened as she finished her sentence. She stared at Stephanie.

"Are you thinking what I'm thinking?" Stephanie asked.

"I think I'm afraid to find out," D.J. answered.

"Tell me," Michelle demanded.

"Well, we all miss Dad, right?" Stephanie asked.

D.J. nodded. "Everything is falling apart around here without him. Jesse and Joey are always busy cleaning up messes or figuring out how to cook or do laundry. . . ."

"And Aunt Becky is working so hard that she's never home!" Michelle put in. "I hate it without Dad here."

"So we all want Dad to come home for good?" Stephanie asked.

Her sisters nodded.

"Then I think I know what to do." Stephanie put her arms around Michelle and D.J.'s shoulders. "Okay, you guys," she whispered. "Here's my plan!"

CHAPTER
12

◆ ◀ ◆ ◆

"This meeting of the John Muir Middle School Student Council will now come to order," Mrs. Booth announced.

"Our first student council meeting!" Allie whispered, squirming in her seat. "Isn't this exciting?"

Stephanie shot a quick glance at Mrs. Booth. Somehow, Stephanie didn't think she approved of squirming. Mrs. Booth seemed like someone you did not want to mess around with.

"Hold still, Allie. We don't want to act like we're new members here," Stephanie whispered.

"But we *are* new," Allie protested.

"Stephanie, Allie," Mrs. Booth broke in. "Something you'd like to share with the rest of us?"

"We were just saying how exciting it is to be here, Mrs. Booth," Stephanie answered quickly.

Mrs. Booth actually smiled at that. "I'm pleased to hear you say so," she said. "I hope you've come prepared to work hard."

"Definitely," Allie assured her.

Mrs. Booth opened an enormous rule book with a snap.

"All right, let's get under way," the adviser said.

The council meeting started with introductions. Then Mrs. Booth handed everyone a copy of the council rules of conduct. Then she handed out the dates and times of all the meetings for the entire school year.

"Here's the agenda for today's meeting," Mrs. Booth said as yet another sheet of paper made its way around the table.

"My dad would totally love this," Stephanie murmured to Allie. "Mrs. Booth is so organized!"

"The first item on our agenda is deciding which issue to bring before the student body—evaluating teachers, or school uniforms. Would anyone care to begin the discussion?" Mrs. Booth asked the group.

"I can't believe the school board is even considering uniforms," Jennifer Sheridan, one of the other class presidents, spoke up right away. "It's out of the Dark Ages."

"Oh, Jennifer," Kevin Carlson, a vice president, protested. "It is not. Get a life."

"We will treat our fellow officers with respect during meetings, Kevin," Mrs. Booth interrupted sternly.

"Sorry," Kevin mumbled. "But I still don't think it's as bad as she says. I think we ought to talk about grading teachers first. That's way more important."

Jennifer and Kevin argued back and forth.

Wow. Student council is sort of boring, Stephanie thought. *It's not nearly as much fun as a Scribe TV meeting.*

That reminded her. She flipped her notebook open and stared thoughtfully at a blank page. Now that the campaign was over, she had lots of catching up to do. Particularly on her work for *The Scribe* and Scribe TV.

Her duties as a producer of Scribe TV were her favorite part of school. But she hadn't even been to the Scribe TV office since the campaign started. If she didn't come up with some great stories fast, Susan Allen would scoop her for the rest of the year.

Stephanie uncapped her pen. She began to brainstorm a list of story ideas.

She was really into a piece on the school's recycling program when Mrs. Booth's voice interrupted her thoughts.

"We'll start the vote with you, Stephanie."

Stephanie's head jerked up. Everyone at the council table was staring at her.

They expected her to cast her vote. But she'd been so busy with her list for Scribe TV, she hadn't heard a thing!

Stephanie took a deep breath.

Calm down, she told herself. *How tough can it be? You either vote yes or no, right?*

"I vote yes, Mrs. Booth," she said confidently.

A ripple of laughter ran around the student council table.

"Stephanie," Mrs. Booth said. She frowned and her chin looked even pointier. "Haven't you been listening?"

"Actually," Allie put in before Stephanie had a chance to answer, "I think I know what Stephanie's trying to say. It shouldn't be either-or. We should put *both* issues before the student body at the same time. That way they can decide which one they think is most important."

Allie gave Stephanie a light kick under the table. "Isn't that right?" she asked.

"Absolutely," Stephanie said.

She breathed a silent sigh of relief. Allie had come through for her again.

Mrs. Booth stared at Stephanie for another moment. "That's a very good suggestion," the adviser said finally. "Officers, your assignment is to poll your classmates about which issue they think is more important—school uniforms or grading teachers. Bring the results to our next meeting."

Mrs. Booth shut her rule book with a snap. "If there's nothing else . . ."

None of the officers said a word.

"This meeting is now adjourned."

"Thanks, Al," Stephanie whispered as she gathered up her books. "You just saved me from total humiliation."

"What were you daydreaming about?" Allie asked.

"Scribe TV stories," Stephanie admitted. "Now that the election is over, I have to start paying more attention to that. Plus, I have to think about Operation Bring Danny Tanner Home. D.J. and Michelle and I are planning a disaster for tonight."

"Well, just be careful," Allie said. "If you don't pay attention in council meetings, your whole presidency will be a disaster!"

"Okay, you guys know what to do, right?" Stephanie asked that afternoon.

She had gathered her sisters in the laundry room

off the kitchen. At exactly four-fifteen they were expecting a call from their father.

It was four-ten—time for phase one of Operation Bring Home Danny Tanner.

"I still don't like the idea of tricking Uncle Jesse," D.J. said.

"I don't like it either, Deej," Stephanie said. "But we all agreed we had to start somewhere. Uncle Jesse is clueless about laundry. This opportunity is too good to pass up."

"I guess you're right," D.J. said.

"Shh," Michelle put in. "He's coming."

Uncle Jesse burst into the laundry room. He carried a basket filled with dirty clothes.

"I really appreciate this, you guys," he said. "I don't understand why I can't get the hang of this laundry thing."

He plunked the basket down on the floor. Stephanie opened the washing machine.

"Let's start with a review of basic laundry procedures, Uncle Jesse," she said. "Once we go over those, I'm sure everything will make much more sense."

"Okay by me," Uncle Jesse agreed. He took up a position between Stephanie and D.J.

Stephanie scooped out a little plastic cup full of detergent. "First, you put the soap in," she instructed.

"No way," D.J. objected. Jesse's head swiveled toward her in confusion. As soon as his head turned, Stephanie dumped the soap into the washing machine.

"You put the clothes in first, Stephanie," D.J. said.

She grabbed a pile of laundry and dumped it into the washer before Uncle Jesse had a chance to notice there was soap in the machine.

"Now you put the soap in," D.J. continued. "When the machine is about half full. That way the soap gets distributed evenly."

"That's not right either," Michelle protested from her position behind Uncle Jesse.

Jesse turned around to face Michelle. D.J. scooped a second cup of soap and dumped it into the machine.

"Wait a minute," Uncle Jesse said. "I thought you guys knew how to do this."

"We do," Michelle assured him. She moved in beside D.J. "First, you load the machine."

Michelle scooped up the rest of the clothes and put them in the washer. "Then you put the soap in, last."

Michelle added a third cup of laundry detergent on top of the clothes. Then she closed the lid. "See, Uncle Jesse?"

"I think so," Jesse answered. But his forehead

wrinkled the way it did whenever he tried to do a difficult section of the daily crossword.

Stephanie snuck a quick look at her watch. It was four-fifteen. Her father should be calling any second.

The phone rang. Instantly, Uncle Jesse's forehead cleared.

"I'll get it," he offered, sprinting for the kitchen.

"Ready?" Stephanie whispered.

"Ready," her sisters answered together.

Stephanie pulled the knob on the washing machine. The laundry room filled with the sound of water pouring into the washer.

"Stand back," Stephanie said. The three girls stepped away from the washing machine.

"Hey, you guys," Uncle Jesse yelled from the kitchen. "Bet you'll never guess who it is. Who wants to talk first?" He stuck his head through the laundry room door, the phone in one hand.

Stephanie put an innocent expression on her face and tried to ignore the thumping sounds coming from the washing machine. She couldn't look at Michelle or D.J. She knew she'd start laughing.

Uncle Jesse's eyes widened as he gazed into the laundry room. "Oh, no!" he exclaimed. "This can't be happening."

The door of the washing machine banged open and a huge stream of soapsuds poured out. Suds covered the machine. Suds covered the floor. The washing machine made loud clanking noises as it churned out more suds.

"Here, here, take this," Jesse cried, thrusting the phone at Stephanie.

"What is going on?" Danny's voice roared in her ear.

"Hi, Dad," Stephanie said.

"Steph," Danny said at once, "tell me what's happening there. What is that noise? What's Jesse yelling about?"

"We're having a small problem with the laundry," Stephanie answered.

"What kind of problem?" Danny practically shouted.

"Um, lots of soap and water rushing out of the washing machine," she replied.

"Well, turn the machine off," Danny bellowed.

Stephanie yanked the phone away from her ear. "Dad says to turn the machine off, Uncle Jesse."

Jesse was staring at the washer as if it were some creature from another planet.

"I can't remember how!" he screamed.

D.J. reached over and turned off the washing machine. The water stopped. The laundry room was quiet except for the soft plop of soapsuds hitting the floor.

And the telephone receiver with Danny's voice

coming out of it, still demanding to know what was going on.

"I just don't understand how a thing like this could have happened," Jesse moaned.

"I don't understand how a thing like that could have happened," Danny's voice said from the phone. "Didn't anybody read my laundry hand-out? If this sort of thing keeps up, I'll have to cut short my assignment and come right home."

Yes! Stephanie thought. *My plan is working!*

She grinned at D.J. and Michelle. "Um, don't worry, Dad," she said. "I think we've got it under control."

You bet we have, she thought as she listened to her father's agitated voice.

Just a few more missions in Operation Bring Home Danny Tanner, and her dad would be home, where he belonged.

CHAPTER
13

◆ ◀ ◆ ◆

"Are you okay, Steph?" Allie asked. "It's only our second student council meeting. I want us to make a good impression this time."

Stephanie pulled out a chair at the council table. She glanced at her watch. The truth was, she had almost forgotten about the meeting. She was so busy planning household disasters and working on her piece for Scribe TV that she'd hardly thought about student council at all.

"Sure I'm okay," Stephanie answered, pulling off her backpack. "Why?"

The heavy backpack slipped through her fingers and crashed to the floor. Papers scattered every which way. When Stephanie bent to pick them up, her pen fell out of her pocket.

"That's why," Allie said. "You've been like that all week."

"It's nothing," Stephanie mumbled, trying to get her stuff picked up before anyone noticed what a klutz she was.

The truth was, Stephanie was pretty tired. Operation Bring Home Danny Tanner took up a lot of her energy.

Every single day, some bizarre incident happened at the Tanner house. Each and every one of them had been reported to Danny. And each and every time they had to clean up the disasters they created!

Danny didn't know the disasters were on purpose, of course. And he'd come closer and closer to completely freaking out.

One day, the timer on the oven hadn't gone off, so dinner burned and the family had to eat cold cereal.

Another day, Comet got out and chased the neighbor's new cat up a tree. They had to call the fire department to get the cat down.

Then, last night, the TV had come on in the middle of the night. It woke the whole house up. Nobody knew how *that* had happened, naturally.

Stephanie yawned as she finished gathering up her papers. It took work planning these "accidents."

"Are you ready for the meeting?" Allie asked.

"Uh, I think so," Stephanie replied. In home-room this morning, she had remembered to ask a few classmates which of the two issues was more important to them.

I'm sure that will be enough, she thought as she slid into her seat. Today's meeting would probably just be another boring debate between Jennifer and Kevin.

Mrs. Booth called the meeting to order. "We'll now review the results of the polls you conducted during the past few days. Would anyone care to begin?" the adviser asked.

Jennifer stood right up. "I would, Mrs. Booth," she said. She opened a thick folder. Inside was a pile of handouts. They were stapled together. Not only that, they were color coded.

Uh-oh, Stephanie thought. *Jennifer really went all out.*

"Here are the results of a questionnaire I passed out each day during lunch break," Jennifer said.

She distributed the handouts.

"Each day has a different colored top sheet," Jennifer went on. "I told students their names wouldn't be used in the results, but I asked them to sign their answers. That way, I could make sure there weren't any duplicates."

"Very nice work, Jennifer," Mrs. Booth compli-mented her.

Jennifer shot a triumphant glance at Kevin. "Thank you," she said.

She sat down. Kevin went next.

"Since this was a student council assignment," he said, "I decided to poll my classmates during political science class."

Kevin had handouts, too. His were in folders.

I am in really big trouble, Stephanie realized. She hadn't paid much attention to the student council assignment. But the other presidents had given it top priority.

"And what about your results, Stephanie?" Mrs. Booth asked.

"I'm afraid I was a little more, um, informal in my approach, Mrs. Booth," Stephanie stammered.

She felt her cheeks grow warm.

There's no way out, she thought. *I'm going to have to admit I'm not prepared.*

Stephanie heard a rustling of papers at her elbow.

"I handled the more formal aspects of our poll," Allie said.

A stack of papers appeared on the table in front of Stephanie. Each section was held together with a giant colored paper clip.

The top page showed a pie chart divided into two sections, colored blue and pink.

"As you can see, the responses have been tallied

by gender," Allie explained. "I thought it was interesting that more boys responded negatively to the idea of school uniforms than girls did."

"Guess our individuality felt more threatened," Kevin quipped.

All the class officers chuckled.

Stephanie felt her blush fade as Allie continued the presentation. What a relief! Allie was totally awesome, just like she'd been at the debate.

She's really into this stuff, Stephanie thought. *Thank goodness!*

Stephanie smiled as she watched her best friend. But then a new thought crept into her head.

Why wasn't she as excited by the student council as Allie was? She was the president. But, so far, all she'd done was drop the ball.

I've been distracted with the mess at home, she told herself. *That's all.*

She was careful to pay close attention during the rest of the meeting.

"Thanks, Allie," she whispered as the meeting broke up. "That was the most awesome save on record."

Allie didn't answer. Her eyes looked kind of troubled.

"Al?" Stephanie said as she followed her friend out of the council room. "Really—thanks."

"Steph," Allie finally said. "I think we have to talk."

"Aren't we doing that right now?" Stephanie joked.

Allie didn't even crack a smile. She just kept walking down the hall.

"Come on," Stephanie said. "I was only teasing."

Allie stopped.

"I just don't understand you, Stephanie," she said. "That's three times I've had to bail you out now."

"I said thank you," Stephanie protested.

"I know," Allie answered. "And I appreciate it. But that's not the point."

"What *is* the point?"

"The point is I shouldn't have had to rescue you in the first place!" Allie cried.

Stephanie's stomach began to feel funny. Allie was right. Not only that, she seemed really upset.

"Taking that survey was your responsibility, Steph," Allie said. "Your responsibility as class president."

"I know," Stephanie began. "But—"

"You were the one who wanted to be president so much. You were the one who wouldn't drop out of the race for anything," Allie interrupted. "Now you don't even pay attention in student

council meetings. So far you haven't done one single thing as president."

"I've been busy," Stephanie said.

"That's no excuse," Allie replied. "I'm only the
vice president. It wasn't my assignment. But I
knew you weren't going to do that survey, so I
did. Someone has to be responsible."

Stephanie looked down at her shoes. She knew
Allie was right. She was so into her stories for
Scribe TV and Operation Danny that she didn't
bother to make time for anything else. Not even
her work for student council.

"I'm not going to bail you out anymore, Steph,"
Allie said quietly. "You wanted to be president. So
be president."

She walked away, leaving Stephanie staring
after her.

Be president, Allie had said. *The only trouble is,
I'm not sure I want to be president.* She groaned out
loud. *What have I gotten myself into?*

CHAPTER
14

◆ ◀ ◆ ◆

"But I want cereal for breakfast," Nicky wailed. His lower lip trembled. He looked ready to burst into tears.

"Me, too!" Alex's face was a mirror image of his brother's.

Stephanie stared at them both in dismay. "Guys, this is no way to start a Monday morning!" she cried.

Operation Bring Home Danny Tanner was going strong. But the family was beginning to fall apart. Even Stephanie was feeling the effects.

The latest disaster was a genuine accident. Someone had left the jug of milk out overnight. This morning it was spoiled. There was no milk for anyone's breakfast.

"Your dad ran to the store," Stephanie told the twins. "He'll bring milk for you in a few minutes."

"We want it now!" Nicky screamed.

Stephanie opened the bread box. "Look! There's half a loaf of bread. How about some toast, you guys?"

"Or Twinkies," Michelle offered, coming into the kitchen. "I think there are still some around."

"No!" Alex screamed, shaking his head. "I want Cheerios."

"We want Cheerios!" Nicky echoed.

Stephanie began to feel a little desperate. Where was Joey?

"There's lots of my campaign candy left," she offered, opening the cupboard where Danny kept his coffee beans. It was filled with open bags of candy. "You guys can pick out your favorite colors."

"I'm tired of sugar breakfast," Nicky said. "I want regular breakfast."

"Cheerios!" Alex yelled.

"Okay, okay," Stephanie said, setting the box on the breakfast table. "We can do Cheerios. We just can't do milk."

Alex stared at the cereal box, his mouth puckering.

"I want Uncle Danny to come home," he wailed. "I want an Uncle Danny breakfast."

Instantly, Nicky's mouth puckered just like his brother's. "I want an Uncle Danny breakfast, too," he cried.

The telephone rang. Stephanie picked it up.

"Hello?" she said.

"Hello, Madam President," her father greeted her.

"We want Uncle Danny breakfast!" Alex and Nicky wailed.

"What's happening?" Danny asked. "Sounds like somebody's kind of upset."

"The twins are having a bad morning," Stephanie answered. "The milk went bad. Unfortunately, the boys have their hearts set on Cheerios for breakfast."

"That's terrible," Danny exclaimed. "Eating a proper breakfast is so important. Doesn't anybody have a backup plan?"

"Uh, not right now," Stephanie answered. *Except for the fact that Jesse went to buy more milk!* "But I'm sure we'll come up with something soon," she added.

"Something with protein," Danny instructed.

"Okay," she replied, smiling. The twins' tantrum was turning into part of the operation!

Stephanie decided it was time to hand the phone over. "Here's Michelle," she said. "Talk to you tomorrow, Dad."

"Okay, honey," Danny said. Stephanie thought it was his most worried tone yet.

Michelle talked to Danny while Stephanie convinced the twins to take some toast with crunchy peanut butter. Then she headed off to collect her things for school.

She was feeling good for the first time since last week's near disaster at the student council meeting.

If her father's reaction to the breakfast problem was anything to go by, Stephanie was willing to bet he'd be home any day.

Once Dad's back for good, I'll be able to concentrate more on things at school, she thought. *Like my Scribe TV stories. And my homework.*

Out of the corner of her eye, Stephanie caught sight of the president's trophy in the center of the mantel.

And the student council, she added. *I have got to get this president thing under control!*

"Steph," Allie exclaimed as Stephanie slid into her homeroom seat. "What on earth are you wearing?"

Stephanie looked down at her soft, faded jeans and flannel shirt. Her favorite comfort clothes. She'd needed them after the stress of breakfast that morning.

"What's the matter?" she asked. "I wear this all the time."

Then Stephanie noticed something strange. Allie was wearing a dress. And shoes with little heels. And panty hose. Allie never dressed like that unless she was going somewhere fancy with her parents.

"What are *you* wearing?" Stephanie asked. "Why are you dressed up?"

Allie just stared at her with wide eyes.

"Come on," Stephanie said, deciding her friend was playing some kind of joke on her. "Quit clowning around."

"It's not a joke," Allie said in a serious voice. "Please don't tell me you forgot."

"Of course I didn't forget," Stephanie assured her. "Forget what?"

Allie groaned. "You *did* forget, didn't you? Today's the day the mayor is coming."

Stephanie felt as if she'd been punched in the stomach.

"But it can't be today," she protested. "It's next week. Mrs. Booth said so."

"She said that last week, Steph," Allie said. "Next week is now *this week.*"

"Oh, no," Stephanie whispered. "I can't believe I spaced on something like this!" She dropped her head into her hands.

The mayor of San Francisco was coming to Muir to meet the student council. Scribe TV was going to broadcast the whole event. Each class president would have the chance to ask Mayor Brown one question.

Stephanie had forgotten all about it. She was completely unprepared.

Not only that, she looked it. Everybody knew you wore your very best clothes to meet the mayor. You didn't wear your oldest jeans and a flannel shirt, even if they were your favorites.

"How soon will the mayor be here?" Stephanie asked desperately. Maybe there was time to go home and change.

"In about five minutes," Allie said, consulting her watch. "Right after homeroom."

"That's it," Stephanie said. "I'm doomed."

Five minutes wasn't enough time to do anything except to prepare for total humiliation.

"I don't even have a question for the mayor," Stephanie said miserably. "My mind is totally frozen."

Allie quickly looked away. Stephanie sighed. She knew that Allie could probably think of a dozen good questions.

Stephanie couldn't ask for any more help. She was on her own this time. No more bailouts. Allie had made that clear.

113

The bell rang.

"Well," Stephanie said, standing up. "I might as well get this over with."

Darcy and Maura were waiting in the hall. They both looked shocked when they saw what Stephanie was wearing.

"Don't even ask," she warned them before they could say a word. "I got so wrapped up in family stuff that I completely forgot about the mayor."

"Maybe it's not so bad," Darcy said as they joined the crowd walking toward the auditorium.

"Darcy's right," Maura put in. "Mayor Brown is cool. Maybe he'll like it that you're sort of casual. Maybe he'll think it shows you're comfortable meeting him."

"Uh-huh," Stephanie said. "Or maybe he'll just think I'm from another planet."

The auditorium was packed by the time they got there. Stephanie saw most of the other council members sitting in a row of chairs on the stage. They all wore dress-up clothes, she noted glumly.

Stephanie saw Susan Allen talking things over with a Scribe TV camera operator.

"Why does the reporter have to be Susan?" she murmured. "This has got to be the worst day of my life."

Stephanie was about to humiliate herself in front

of the entire student body. And Susan was going to get the whole thing on tape.

Stephanie would never be able to live this down. Ever.

"Okay, Steph," Allie said in a low voice. "Let's go."

Silently, Stephanie followed Allie up to the stage and sat down. She avoided looking at Mrs. Booth. She knew the council adviser would be furious with her for dressing so casually.

"At least I'm first," Stephanie murmured to Allie as Mr. Bird introduced the mayor. "I can get my humiliation over with quickly."

"Your first question comes from Stephanie Tanner," the principal said. He gestured for Stephanie to stand up.

Stephanie cleared her throat. She was so nervous that her ears were ringing. She still didn't have a clue about what to ask the mayor.

Mayor Brown smiled at Stephanie.

How does he do that? she thought. *How does he stay so relaxed?*

"What's the hardest thing about being mayor?" she blurted out.

His smile got a little bigger. "Coming up with good answers to all the questions I'm asked," he joked.

His answer got a chuckle from the audience. But it didn't make Stephanie feel any better.

She stood onstage in her oldest, sloppiest clothes as Mayor Brown went on to talk about the importance of organizing your responsibilities.

That's just what I haven't done, Stephanie thought. *And now the whole world knows it.*

She could see the red light on the Scribe TV camera pointed right at her. It was an absolute nightmare.

Finally, the mayor finished with Stephanie's question. He shook her hand. She returned to her seat.

The rest of the question-and-answer session passed in a dismal blur. *I'm all wrong for this*, Stephanie thought. *In fact, I HATE THIS.*

Running for president had been a great experience. *Being* president wasn't wonderful at all.

I was concentrating so much on winning the election, I never thought about what would happen after I was elected, Stephanie realized.

Now it was too late to think about it.

I'm trapped! she thought. *Trapped for an entire year's worth of miserable student council meetings.*

And there was absolutely nothing she could do about it.

CHAPTER
15

◆ ◂ ▸ ◆

"Okay, Stephanie. Spill," Maura commanded. "You've hardly said a word since the mayor's visit this morning. What's wrong?"

Stephanie sighed. Maura had been nice enough to walk home with her after school, even though Stephanie knew she was bad company today.

"It's so embarrassing," Stephanie moaned. "But I suppose I should be used to that after this morning."

Maura plopped down onto the living room couch. "I'm all ears," she said.

"I'm the worst class president in the history of the world," Stephanie burst out.

"Today wasn't one of your better moments, I'll admit," Maura said. "But things aren't quite that bad."

"No," Stephanie said. "They're worse. The truth is, I'm all wrong for president."

"What makes you say that?" Maura asked.

"I'm not interested in it," Stephanie admitted. "I thought being president would be exciting. But so far all I've done is sit through a bunch of boring meetings."

"And you humiliated yourself in public," Maura added, joking.

Stephanie sighed. "You may be kidding, Maura. But it's true. I just proved that I'm all wrong for the job. But it doesn't make any difference how I feel. I'm trapped."

Maura was silent for a moment. "Maybe you're too close to the problem," she said at last. "Back up a little. Think about what made you decide to run for president in the first place. That might help you get your enthusiasm back."

Stephanie closed her eyes and tried to picture the exact moment she'd decided to run for office. Instantly, the image of the president's trophy popped into her mind.

She opened her eyes and gasped. She stared at the trophy sitting on the mantel, and at D.J.'s dean's list certificate next to it.

"D.J.'s award!" she exclaimed. "That's how it started. Everyone was making a big fuss over D.J. for winning her award. And talking about what special things I was doing, and the only special thing in my life was the election." She frowned.

"I don't get it," Maura said.

"Well, somehow everything got turned around," Stephanie said. "D.J. and my dad said I shouldn't write about the election, I should be part of it. Then you said the same thing, and I saw the trophy, and . . ."

"Now I see," Maura said. "We all pushed you to run. And then you got into winning."

"That's exactly right," Stephanie agreed. "I *never* ran for the right reasons. I jumped in because everyone told me I could win. I did it all for that big, shiny trophy!"

She shook her head in disbelief, thinking it all over.

"Wow. That's amazing," Maura said. "Do you feel better now that you know the truth?"

"I'm not sure yet," Stephanie admitted. "I'm still the class president, like it or not."

"Don't worry," Maura said. "I'm sure you'll think of something."

"Thanks, Maura," Stephanie said. "But I don't need to *think* of something. I need to *do* something about this situation."

Stephanie stared thoughtfully at her trophy. "The question is, *what?*"

* * *

Brrriiinnggg!

Stephanie rolled over and smacked the alarm clock.

"No two ways about it," she muttered. "No sensible person gets up at six-thirty A.M."

Particularly when all they have to look forward to is another awful student council meeting.

Stephanie eased her feet out of bed. She sucked in a quick breath as her toes touched the cold floor.

A delicious smell filled her nostrils.

I must still be asleep and dreaming, she thought as she hunted for her slippers. *That smells just like bacon frying.*

Stephanie knew that was impossible. Joey was in charge of breakfast. He was lucky to get a cereal box open.

She pulled on her bathrobe and headed for the hall. Michelle was still sound asleep. She always slept right through the alarm clock.

I'll wake her up in a minute, Stephanie decided. She opened the bedroom door. The smell overwhelmed her. Stephanie stopped.

She took one sniff. Then another.

Bacon, definitely. But there was something more. Something that smelled like cake but wasn't.

Muffins, Stephanie thought.

Super-deluxe-extra-energy muffins, to be exact. Nothing else smelled quite like them.

Smelling super-deluxe-extra-energy muffins could mean only one thing.

Her father was home!

Stephanie raced downstairs to the kitchen. Danny stood by the stove. He wore the Kiss the Cook apron that the twins had given him for Christmas.

"Dad!" Stephanie exclaimed, throwing her arms around him in a big hug. "I'm so glad you're home!"

Danny hugged her back. Then he took the bacon off the stove.

"I'm glad, too," he said. "Traveling was fun, but—"

"There's no place like home!" Stephanie finished for him.

"And there's nothing like my home-brewed coffee," Danny went on. "Boy, I really missed this stuff."

He reached to open the cupboard where he kept his coffee beans.

"Dad!" Stephanie cried out. "Wait! Don't!"

Startled, Danny jerked on the cupboard door. The half-open bags of Skooters tipped over. Pieces of the brightly colored candy spilled and bounced all over the kitchen floor.

Stephanie groaned. "Oh, no!"

Danny put his hands on his hips as he watched the candy roll everywhere. He didn't say anything until the last piece stopped moving.

"You guys really *do* need me," he said, his eyes twinkling. "In a big way. I guess it's a good thing I quit my assignment."

Stephanie's breath caught in her throat. She stared at her father. "You *quit?*" she cried. "Tell me you're joking!"

CHAPTER
16

◆ ◢ ◆ ◆

Stephanie stared at her father. "We never wanted you to quit," she exclaimed.

"Well, it was the only way I could get here fast enough," Danny said. "But I'm glad I did. Nothing's in the right place around here. Now I understand why so many things went wrong."

Stephanie walked to the table and collapsed onto a chair. Suddenly she didn't feel so well.

"Dad, there's something I have to tell you," she said. "I think you'd better sit down."

Danny looked puzzled as he sat down. "Okay," he said. "What's on your mind?"

Stephanie swallowed hard. "You know all those disasters that happened?" she asked.

Danny nodded.

"Well, some of them weren't exactly by accident," Stephanie admitted. "D.J., Michelle, and I planned them."

"You did?" Danny looked startled. "But why?"

"Because we wanted you to come home," Stephanie said. "Nothing was going right when you were gone. The house was a mess. Meals were awful. So we—" She hesitated.

"You what?" Danny prompted.

Stephanie took a deep breath. "Well, we thought that if *you* thought we couldn't get along without you . . ."

Stephanie's voice trailed off. Danny finished the sentence for her.

"Then I would hurry home."

"Right." Stephanie felt miserable. Danny was quiet for a moment. Stephanie couldn't tell if he was mad or not.

"Thank you for telling me the truth, Stephanie," he finally said.

"You're not mad, are you?"

"Yes," Danny said. Stephanie felt even worse.

"And no," her father went on. "I'm touched that you girls wanted me to come home so much. But I wish you'd just told me that."

Stephanie nodded. "It's what we should have done. It's just that things were so awful around here. And the worst part was, well, when I got elected president—I hated it the whole time," she blurted out.

"Hated it?" Danny looked stunned.

Stephanie explained everything. How she jumped into the election for all the wrong reasons. How she never enjoyed performing her duties. How much she wished she'd never run in the first place.

"I feel terrible," Danny said when she finished. "You know, Steph, a lot of this is my fault," he added. "I didn't take the time to listen to you. I'm the one who got caught up in the excitement of winning trophies and elections. I practically ordered you to run."

"But I went along with it," Stephanie told him.

"I should have stopped you," Danny said. "Winning prizes isn't a reason to do something. It's a reward for doing them well. The only reason to run for president is because you want to *be* president."

"That sounds familiar," Stephanie admitted. "It's what Allie said." She told her dad how Allie felt the exact same way. "Now I see that Allie would have made a much better president than me," she finished. "But there's nothing I can do about it."

Danny gave her a big hug. "I'm sorry, Steph," he told her. "I really let you down. I'll try to make up for it, now that I'm back. In a way, I'm glad I don't have to go to work for a while."

"Your job!" Stephanie moaned. "Don't remind me. You weren't supposed to quit your job, Dad. We just wanted you to come home."

Danny chuckled. "I didn't quit my whole job, Stephanie," he replied. "I just quit the rest of this assignment."

"Really?" she asked.

"Yup." Danny stood up. "Those muffins will be ready in just a few minutes," he told Stephanie. "I'd appreciate it if you'd take them out of the oven."

"Sure, Dad," Stephanie said. "But where will you be?"

"In my office," Danny answered. "I have to make a phone call. I need to talk to my boss about finishing the rest of my assignment. It will take only another day or two."

"That's a good idea, Dad," Stephanie said, her spirits lifting.

Danny smiled. "Well, you know, I didn't like being away from you guys either." He ruffled her hair. "Back in a minute," he promised as he left the kitchen.

Stephanie waited for the muffins to finish baking.

Dad sure made his decision quickly, she thought.

And it can't be easy for him to tell his boss that he changed his mind.

But he was doing it anyway.

And that's what I have to do, Stephanie realized.

No matter how hard it was, she had to tell everyone that she had changed her mind.

I'll do it, too, she vowed. *I just hope I have the nerve!*

CHAPTER
17

♦ ◂ ◗ ♦

"This meeting will now come to order."

Stephanie sat nervously in student council. In just a few minutes, she'd begin Operation Make Things Right.

My third and final operation, Stephanie promised herself. *But I bet I saved the best for last.*

Stephanie reached out with her foot and rested it on her backpack. The feel of the big lump beneath her feet gave her a boost of courage.

Mrs. Booth handed out the agenda for that afternoon's meeting. Quickly, Stephanie raised her hand.

"I have an item I'd like to bring before the council, Mrs. Booth," she said.

The adviser's pointed eyebrows drew together in

a frown. "This is a little unusual, Stephanie," she said. "If you wanted to discuss something at this meeting, you were supposed to tell me at the last meeting. Can it wait?"

"I'm sorry," Stephanie said. "But it's really important that we discuss this *now.*"

Mrs. Booth studied her for a moment. "Very well."

Stephanie stood up and took a deep breath. *Here I go*, she thought. *It's now or never.*

"I'd like to step down as class president."

The student council room was silent.

"This is highly unusual," Mrs. Booth commented.

"Can she do that?" Jennifer Sheridan asked.

The adviser looked thoughtful. "It's almost unheard of, but, yes, she can. I hope you intend to explain your reasons, Stephanie."

"I do."

"Go ahead," Mrs. Booth said.

Stephanie took another deep breath. "During my campaign, I talked about school spirit. I think my class has a lot to offer. We could really make a big contribution to the school. But only if we have a strong leader. Someone who can organize responsibilities, just like the mayor said. I thought I could be that leader. But now I know I can't."

Out of the corner of her eye, Stephanie stole a quick glance at Allie.

"Fortunately," Stephanie continued, "I know someone who can. Someone who's already shown her commitment to the student council."

"But you'd be *quitting*," Kevin Carlson put in.

"I don't think of it as quitting," Stephanie said. "I think of it as making a new decision—the decision that's right for my class. They should have the strongest leadership possible. That's why I want to step down—in favor of Allie Taylor."

Allie gasped.

The other council members burst into applause.

"The council will have to vote on this," Mrs. Booth said when the clapping had stopped.

"Of course," Stephanie said. She sat back down.

"Stephanie, are you absolutely sure?" Allie whispered.

"Absolutely positively, Allie," Stephanie said. "You were the best candidate all along."

The council voted Allie in by a unanimous show of hands.

"Thank you," Allie said. "I'll try to earn your confidence."

Stephanie reached down and pulled the president's trophy out of her backpack.

"Congratulations, Madam President," she told Allie. "You deserved this trophy more than I did. And it's time I admitted that—to *everyone*."

*   *   *

"Boy, something sure smells good," she called as she entered her kitchen that afternoon. She grinned as she joined Danny at the oven. "What did you do, spend all day in here?"

"Just about," Danny said. He spread a dollop of frosting on a layer cake. "Here and the laundry room."

"Please don't mention laundry," Stephanie begged.

Danny laughed. He got out a package of Oreo cookies. He put several in a plastic bag. Then he whacked them with a rolling pin. He sprinkled the crumbled cookies on top of a frosted white cake.

"Hey," Stephanie said, suddenly realizing what her dad was doing. "You're making my favorite cake."

"Of course I am," Danny said. "We never really got to celebrate your big win."

Stephanie felt her cheeks flush. "But I'm not president anymore, Dad. Don't you remember? I gave the trophy back."

Danny finished frosting the cake.

"Dad, didn't you hear me?" she asked. "I gave it back. I'm not president anymore. I resigned in favor of Allie."

"I heard you," Danny said. He lifted the cake on a tray.

"Hey, what's going on around here?" Jesse

131

poked his head into the kitchen. "I thought we were having a celebration."

Stephanie shook her head. "There's no reason to celebrate now, Uncle Jesse."

"You're wrong about that, Steph," her father told her. "Now follow me."

Stephanie walked behind him into the living room.

The whole family was gathered around the coffee table.

"Three cheers for Stephanie!" Joey yelled as she appeared.

Stephanie's mouth dropped open in surprise. "What's going on?" she asked. "We're not really celebrating anything."

"Yes, we are," Danny said. "We're celebrating *you*, Steph."

"We all heard what you did today. And it took a lot of courage," Becky told her.

"And perseverance," Michelle added. Everyone laughed.

"Hey! Isn't it time to sing 'For She's a Jolly Good Fellow'?" D.J. asked.

Everyone started singing.

This is the greatest, Stephanie thought. *This is exactly the celebration I wanted all along. And I didn't have to win a thing!*

FULL HOUSE™

SISTERS

A brand-new series starring Stephanie AND Michelle!

#1 Two On The Town

Stephanie and Michelle find themselves
in the big city—and in big trouble!

#2 One Boss Too Many

Stephanie and Michelle think camp will be major fun.
If only these two sisters were getting along!

When sisters get together...expect the unexpected!

A MINSTREL® BOOK

Published by Pocket Books

2012-01

FULL HOUSE™
Michelle

#5: THE GHOST IN MY CLOSET 53573-0/$3.99
#6: BALLET SURPRISE 53574-9/$3.99
#7: MAJOR LEAGUE TROUBLE 53575-7/$3.99
#8: MY FOURTH-GRADE MESS 53576-5/$3.99
#9: BUNK 3, TEDDY, AND ME 56834-5/$3.99
#10: MY BEST FRIEND IS A MOVIE STAR!
(Super Edition) 56835-3/$3.99
#11: THE BIG TURKEY ESCAPE 56836-1/$3.99
#12: THE SUBSTITUTE TEACHER 00364-X/$3.99
#13: CALLING ALL PLANETS 00365-8/$3.99
#14: I'VE GOT A SECRET 00366-6/$3.99
#15: HOW TO BE COOL 00833-1/$3.99
#16: THE NOT-SO-GREAT OUTDOORS 00835-8/$3.99
#17: MY HO-HO-HORRIBLE CHRISTMAS 00836-6/$3.99
MY AWESOME HOLIDAY FRIENDSHIP BOOK
(An Activity Book) 00840-4/$3.99
FULL HOUSE MICHELLE OMNIBUS 02181-8/$6.99
#18: MY ALMOST PERFECT PLAN 00837-4/$3.99
#19: APRIL FOOLS 01729-2/$3.99
#20: MY LIFE IS A THREE-RING CIRCUS 01730-6/$3.99
#21: WELCOME TO MY ZOO 01731-4/$3.99
#22: THE PROBLEM WITH PEN PALS 01732-2/$3.99
#23: MERRY CHRISTMAS, WORLD! 02098-6/$3.99

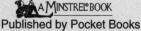

Published by Pocket Books

Simon & Schuster Mail Order Dept. BWB
200 Old Tappan Rd., Old Tappan, N.J. 07675

Please send me the books I have checked above. I am enclosing $_____ (please add $0.75 to cover the postage and handling for each order. Please add appropriate sales tax). Send check or money order--no cash or C.O.D.'s please. Allow up to six weeks for delivery. For purchase over $10.00 you may use VISA: card number, expiration date and customer signature must be included.

Name _____

Address _____

City _____ State/Zip _____

VISA Card # _____ Exp.Date _____

Signature _____

1033-28

FULL HOUSE Stephanie™

Available from Minstrel® Books Published by Pocket Books

It doesn't matter if you live around the corner...
or around the world...
If you are a fan of Mary-Kate and Ashley Olsen,
you should be a member of

MARY-KATE + ASHLEY'S FUN CLUB™

Here's what you get:
Our Funzine™
An autographed color photo
Two black & white individual photos
A full size color poster
An official **Fun Club**™ membership card
A **Fun Club**™ school folder
Two special **Fun Club**™ surprises
A holiday card
Fun Club™ collectibles catalog
Plus a **Fun Club**™ box to keep everything in

To join Mary-Kate + Ashley's Fun Club™, fill out the form
below and send it along with

U.S. Residents – $17.00
Canadian Residents – $22 U.S. Funds
International Residents – $27 U.S. Funds

MARY-KATE + ASHLEY'S FUN CLUB™
859 HOLLYWOOD WAY, SUITE 275
BURBANK, CA 91505

NAME:_____

ADDRESS:_____

_CITY:_____ STATE:_____ ZIP:_____

PHONE:(____) _____ BIRTHDATE:_____